Dear Reader,

What a delight to be able to share my one and only time travel novel with you again! I've always been intrigued by the idea of going back in time—knowing, of course, everything I know now! When I finally sat down to write a time travel novel, it turned out that, instead of stepping back into the past, I brought my Western heroine into the future.

What made it so much fun was imagining how a nineteenth-century woman would deal with all the modern mechanisms that make our work so much simpler...and our lives so much more complicated. It also gave me an opportunity to focus on how women's rights, women's fashions and women's attitudes have changed over the past century—especially in relation to men! And imagine my hero's surprise when the beautiful woman he rescues turns out to be from another time and place.

Those of you familiar with my HAWK'S WAY series have an extra treasure in store. You'll be seeing the first appearance of Honey Farrell, the heroine of *Honey and the Hired Hand,* and Adam Phillips, the hero of *The Rancher and the Runaway Bride.* I had no inkling at the time I wrote *A Little Time in Texas* that these characters were destined to have their own books. But what fun to discover they did.

Happy reading!

Joan Johnston

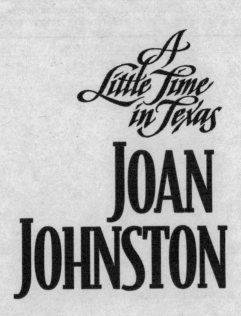

A Little Time in Texas

JOAN JOHNSTON

MIRA®

ISBN 1-55166-629-4

A LITTLE TIME IN TEXAS

Copyright © 1992 by Joan Mertens Johnston.

Visit us at www.mirabooks.com

Printed in U.S.A.

For my sister Jennifer Eloise Wilkes,
who always embraces an adventure

1

Angela Taylor backed away until she came up against a wall of solid rock. She was trapped. She counted the odds. Six to one. Not good. She should have gotten off the road when she'd heard them coming. A woman walking alone was considered easy prey. She told herself to calm down, to breathe deeply. These no-good sidewinders didn't know it, but there was more mettle in her little finger than most women had in their whole bodies. She wasn't about to give up or give in. Her eyes narrowed, her stance widened, and her hands formed into fists. The six men surrounding her might eventually overwhelm her, but they would pay dearly before they did.

"Say there, little lady," one cowboy drawled, "you gonna cooperate, or not?"

"I'm not."

"Ain't hardly enough of her to go around," another cowboy complained.

"Don't like that look on her face," a third said. "Plain mean."

Another laughed. "You scared, Slim? One woman ain't no match for—"

Angel saw the cowboy's mouth drop and his eyes go wide. At almost the same moment a large male hand clamped around her waist and she was jerked completely off her feet. She clawed and bit and kicked, but her captor didn't let go. Angel could have wept when she realized that she'd been caught by such an old trick. There weren't six cowboys. There were *seven!*

Only this one apparently didn't intend to share her with the others. And they weren't too happy about it.

"Hey, there! Where you goin' with her?"

"That girl belongs to all of us! You bring her back here!"

"Hells bells! There's a damned cave in that rock. Look out! He's gettin' away with her!"

"Come on! Let's go after him!"

Angel would have screamed but she couldn't breathe, the seventh man had such a tight hold on her. She struggled mightily in his arms but there was no question of escaping. The arm around her was thick with muscle. From the feel of the hard male body at her back, the rest of him was equally strong. Her feet hadn't touched ground since he'd grabbed her. They were racing deeper and deeper into the cave, through a labyrinth of tunnels in the rock. It was pitch-black, and she had no idea how the cowboy was going to get them back out again.

Suddenly they stopped. There was no sound except the man's harsh breathing and her grunts as she struggled against his strength.

Another fear, even deeper than that of the man, took hold of her. The dark. She was terrified of the dark. Abruptly she stopped struggling. Her breathing was tortured as fear overwhelmed her and held her paralyzed. Her eyes went wide, seeking the light.

There was none.

Angel whimpered, a pitiful, plaintive sound.

"Be still," the seventh man hissed.

But she was in the grip of a terror more powerful than the threat of mere physical harm. The whimper became a low moan.

The kidnapper's hand clamped over her mouth just as one of the cowboys in pursuit passed close enough that she could smell a month's worth of sweat and leather and horse. Angel felt relieved, then horrified as the sound of boots on stone faded into the distance. Better to face six men in the light than one in the dark.

"You see anything?" one of the searching cowboys yelled to another.

"Not a damned thing!"

"We'll never find them in the dark," a third ranted.

"I'm gettin' outta here. This place is spooked," another said.

The voices moved away. They were giving up the hunt. Angel could still hear them. Voices carried in the dark.

"We can't let him get away with stealin' her like that," a cowboy grumbled.

"Who said we're gonna?"

"What's that you got there? Dynamite? What're you gonna do with that?"

"Blow them to Kingdom Come. Or leastwise trap 'em in there till Judgment Day."

"You can't—"

"Who's gonna know? They ain't gonna tell. 'Sides. It'll serve 'em both right. If we can't have her, nobody can."

"I ain't so sure about this," one cowboy said.

By then it was too late. Several sticks of dynamite had been lit and tossed into the cave entrance.

Angel only had a second to acknowledge the fact that they were doomed. Anger flared. She wasn't ready to die trapped in the dark. She wrenched free and started running for the opening of the cave. She had to escape!

She heard her captor swear low and mean as

he chased her. He grunted with effort as he threw himself bodily at her. His forward motion forced her down hard as he covered her with his body.

Mere seconds passed before the first explosion came, followed by a second and a third. The sound was deafening. The repercussions rocked the inside walls of the cave. Angel choked on the settling dust, but only a few pebble-sized rocks fell near them.

"Where the hell did you think you were going?" the man asked as he sat up and brushed himself off.

"I would think that was obvious." Angel tried peering through the gloom. She coughed from the dust. "Do you think we can dig ourselves out of here?"

"Not hardly."

"At least we're alive," she said. "We—"

"Shut up and listen."

"I don't hear—"

He clamped a hand over her mouth, and she heard it. The ominous sound of cracking rock. The man cursed vehemently as a low rumble began, sending a shudder through the cave.

Suddenly he bolted upright and yanked her to her feet. "If you want to live, you'll run. Run like the devil is at your heels!"

He took off in the dark, his hand clamped like

a vise on her wrist. Angel careered after him, her arm stretched out of the socket as her short legs valiantly tried to keep pace with his long strides.

The rumbling sound seemed to follow them, until finally it caught up with them. Angel felt herself being propelled off her feet by a blast of air. With the kind of strength she could only imagine, the seventh man pulled her into the protective circle of his arms before they were both thrown forward.

"Get ready! Here it comes!"

Angel wanted to ask "Here what comes?" but it was already too late for that. There was no way she could have prepared for what followed. Behind them the cave began to collapse. Thousands of tons of rock fell, blocking their way out and sealing them in what had become their tomb.

When the dust settled again, Angel was surprised to realize that she could breathe easily. She wondered how long the air would last…and whether her kidnapper would take advantage of their remaining time alive to take what he had risked both their lives to get.

The man sat up and put a hand on her shoulder. "You okay?"

"Of all the stupid, shallow-pated, lack-wit questions I ever heard, that one—"

"Whoa, there, lady. That's no way to talk to someone who just saved your life."

Angel sat up abruptly, scooting backward out of range of his hand and stared into the dark. She knew he was there, she just couldn't see him. "You have me all to yourself now," she said bitterly. "For all the good it'll do you. I have no intention of relinquishing my virtue to some varmint who—"

"Whoa, there," he said. "I have no designs on your, uh, virtue."

"Then why did you drag me in here?" she demanded.

"I was rescuing you, dammit!"

"*Rescuing* me! In case you hadn't noticed, we're *trapped* in here. We're going to die! We're—"

"Whoa, there, lady."

"If you say that again, I'm going to scream," Angel warned.

When the cowboy chuckled she said, "I'd like to know what you find so funny about this situation. We're going to *die*. We're *trapped*."

"No, we're not."

"I don't know where you've been for the past few minutes. To refresh your memory, this whole cave just came down practically on our heads.

There must be *tons* of rock between us and the only way out of here.''

''That wasn't the only way out.''

Angel was afraid to hope that she'd heard him right. ''What?''

''There's another way out. I've been in this cave before, but I've never come in this direction. Today I wasn't paying attention and I took a wrong turn. I didn't realize there was another way to daylight. You have no idea how surprised I was to see you.'' He whistled long and low. ''Sure looked like you planned to give those cowboys a run for their money.''

''I wouldn't have made it easy for them,'' she agreed. ''You'd best be warned and watch out yourself.''

He laughed then, a rich, full sound. ''Lady, I wouldn't dare make a move on a hellcat like you. By the way, what's your name?''

''Angel.''

That made him laugh again. ''Far as I can tell, you're anything but.''

''Now, look here, Mr.—''

''Name's Dallas. Dallas Masterson. Pleased to meet you, Angel—Angel what?''

''Taylor.''

''Pleased to meet you, Angel Taylor.''

She imagined him tipping his hat. Only she was

pretty sure he wasn't wearing one. "If you know the way out, why are we still sitting here?"

"There is a slight problem."

Angel tensed. "What's that?"

"I lost all my gear back there at the entrance—exit—to the cave. I don't have any light. So while I know there's another way out, we may have a problem finding it in the dark."

Angel had forgotten about the dark. Now the blackness rose again to suffocate her. "Oh, dear God."

"What's wrong?"

"I'm afraid of the dark," Angel whispered.

An instant later strong arms embraced her. Dallas tucked her head down under his chin. As he did so, at least a day's growth of whiskers scraped against her temple. Pressed up so close to him, she could hear his heart thumping against his chest.

"Better?" he murmured.

To Angel's surprise, she did feel better. The dark was not nearly so frightening within the cocoon of warmth he had created.

"How long have you been afraid of the dark?" Dallas asked.

"Since I—" She stiffened in his arms. "That's none of your business. Look, are you going to just sit here, or are we going to try to find the way out?''

He didn't answer with words, simply stood and took her along with him. "Let's go," he said curtly.

Angel heard the irritation in his voice. She hadn't meant to be so rude, but she couldn't explain something so personal to a perfect stranger. Still, she couldn't help feeling grateful when he took her hand in his and didn't let go of it. Of course, he probably only held on because he didn't want to lose track of her in the dark. But she found comfort from the contact, all the same.

"Coming down," he said.

"What?"

"The ceiling's getting lower. Duck your—"

"Ouch!"

"You okay?"

"Of all the dumb, noddy-polled, loplolly questions I ever—"

Dallas chuckled. "You've got a quaint way of expressing yourself, Angel. But I get the message." He reached back and found her hand where she had pressed it to her forehead. "How bad is it?"

"I'll live."

"Good girl." He patted her on the back and

pushed her head lower. "Keep your head down. It gets worse."

So much for sympathy, Angel thought.

He was right, though. Things did get worse. Soon they were crouching, then crawling on their bellies.

"How much farther?" she asked.

"Another hour. Maybe two."

Five minutes more would have been too long. Another hour—or two—seemed an eternity. She was exhausted. There was a hole in the knee of her trousers, and skin was scraping off every time she moved. "Can we stop and rest a minute?"

"There's a place where we can sit, just a little farther on."

That sounded more appealing than stopping on her belly, so Angel kept crawling. A few minutes later they were sitting up across from each other. There wasn't enough room for Angel to stretch out completely, so she sat with her knees upraised. The stone was cool behind her back, and she thanked whoever was responsible for the dry rock floor and the apparent lack of animal life in the cave.

"How could your friends do something like this to you?" Angel asked.

"They weren't my friends."

"Then why did you get involved?" Angel asked.

"It's my job to help damsels in distress."

Angel smiled despite the awfulness of the circumstances. "What are you? A knight in shining armor?"

"No. I'm a Texas Ranger."

"Of all the tom-doodle, gim-crack things I ever heard—why didn't you just say so in the first place?"

"I never got the chance."

"When I think how scared I was of you—and all for nothing."

"Does that mean you aren't scared of me now?"

There was a long pause. "Should I be?"

He snorted. "Not hardly. All I want to do is get you out of here and headed safely home. Then I plan to wash my hands of you and forget I ever met you."

Absurdly, Angel was irritated by his attitude. So, he couldn't wait to get shuck of her. Well, it wasn't any skin off her nose if he did. She would be glad to be shed of him, too.

"What were you doing out there all alone?" he asked.

"Walking."

"Maybe I should have asked where you were headed."

"San Antonio."

"That's quite a walk from the hill country southwest of Austin, especially for a sprite of a woman like you."

"I'm stronger than I look."

"I won't argue with that," he said, chuckling. "It's still a long way for a woman to be walking by herself."

"It's either travel alone or not at all," Angel said.

He paused, then asked, "No husband?"

Angel sighed. "No. No family at all."

The thought of all the walking alone she had yet to do reminded her about her skinned knee. "Do you by any chance have a bandanna?" she asked.

"Sure. Why?"

"My trousers are ripped and my right knee's getting scraped worse every time I move. I wanted to try and bandage it."

"I'll do it."

Before Angel could protest, Dallas had reached for her. Only he missed her knee and found her thigh. She tensed at the touch of his hand. His fingers walked their way down her leg to her knee.

"Found it," he said. "Feels like you skinned it pretty bad."

Angel hissed in a breath of air as his fingers gently probed her wounded knee. She stiffened as he straightened her leg out across his lap and began tying the bandanna in place. She wasn't used to being touched by anyone, and most especially not by a man.

"That ought to do it," Dallas said, patting her leg.

Angel suddenly wished it wasn't so dark. Maybe if she could see the face of this stranger, she wouldn't feel so awkward in his presence. But there wasn't any light and wouldn't be for at least another hour—or two.

"What do you look like?" Angel asked.

There was a long silence. Dallas drew in a breath of air and huffed it out. "I don't know what to say."

"What color eyes do you have?"

"Brown."

"Hair?"

"Brown."

"How would you describe your face?"

"It's just a face," he said curtly.

"You're not being much help!" Angel snapped back.

"What do you want me to say?"

Angel realized it had been foolish to ask him to describe himself. But she was glad he hadn't bragged he was handsome...or admitted he was plain. Still, she was curious.

If the situation were different, she would never have asked; but if the situation were different, she wouldn't have needed to. "Could I touch your face? I think I could tell by feeling, what you look like."

He hesitated so long she was afraid he was going to refuse. At last he said, "All right."

To her surprise he lifted her up and set her on his lap facing him, so her legs straddled his waist. It was a far more intimate pose than she would have liked, but she was afraid to complain lest he withdraw his permission for her examination. She was conscious of her breasts inches from his chest, of the heat of his thighs under hers. She could feel his breath on her face. An uncontrollable shiver ran down her spine.

"Anytime you're ready," he said.

Angel held her breath as she reached out tentatively in the dark. She found his chin. There was a small cleft in it.

"When was the last time you shaved?" she asked, testing the rough bristle of beard under her fingers.

"Three days ago."

She slid her hand along his jaw and felt the muscle work under her hand. It was a strong jaw and led to prominent cheekbones. His nose was straight and not too big, but it had a bump along the bridge.

"What happened here?" she asked.

"Broke it in a fistfight. Twice."

There were wrinkles on his forehead and crow's-feet at the edges of his eyes. He had done some living.

"How old are you?"

"I'll be thirty-four next month. How old are you?"

"A lady never tells her age," she said, then added, "Twenty-two."

He had a widow's peak. His hair was thick and soft, and she let her fingers slide through it all the way down to where it curled over his collar.

"You need a haircut."

"I like it the way it is."

Apparently he was used to getting his own way.

His eyes were wide-set and large, and the lashes were ridiculously long and curled up from his cheeks where they lay. His eyelids were softer than the skin on the rest of his face, which felt not quite smooth, but not leathery, either. The scar on his cheek intrigued her.

"What happened here?"

"Knife fight."

She frowned. "Seems you get into a lot of fights."

"Hazard of the job."

Angel had left his mouth for last, because it seemed the most personal of his features. There were deep slashes on either side of it. She wondered if he dimpled when he smiled.

"Smile for me."

"Why?"

"Please."

What she felt under her hand was more like a grimace, but yes, there were dimples there. "You can relax now," she said.

She felt a genuine smile form under her hands as he said, "Thanks."

His mouth, when he relaxed it, was wide, the lips thin, although the lower lip protruded slightly. She traced it with her fingers and felt him stiffen.

"Does that tickle?"

"No," he said in a husky voice.

Suddenly his hands tightened on her waist.

"Angel?"

She felt his breath on her face, felt him closing the distance between their bodies. What did he want?

"You can tell a lot more about my mouth this way," he said.

Suddenly she felt his lips on hers. Soft. And damp. And insistent. And yes, the bottom lip was full. It was an altogether wonderful mouth.

His tongue brushed against her closed lips, seeking entrance. The feeling was so exquisite that Angel waited for it to come again. His lips teased hers, coaxing. His tongue brushed her mouth again, and she gasped at the pleasure. His tongue slipped inside and retreated just as quickly.

Angel felt her heart pounding; it was hard to catch her breath. She grabbed handfuls of Dallas's shirt.

"Dallas, I—"

His mouth captured hers again. She kept her lips sealed, afraid of what might happen if she relented to his probing tongue. This was all forbidden territory. Virgin territory.

Suddenly Angel realized she was kissing a perfect stranger. She pushed against his chest with the heels of her hands, and her mouth was abruptly released.

Angel had been so wrapped up in her own reactions to the kiss she hadn't noticed what was happening to Dallas. Now that they were no longer kissing, she realized his breathing was as tortured as hers, and his heart was pounding under her fist.

"Did you find out everything you wanted to

know?'' Dallas asked in a voice harsh with re-strained need.

"Yes," Angel gasped.

He set her away from him. "Then I think it's time we got started again."

He headed away from her, and she had no choice but to follow, unless she wanted to be left alone in the dark. To her relief the cave ceiling almost immediately rose again, so they could walk upright. When it did, he reached back for her hand.

"I don't want to lose you now," he said.

"I want to thank you for rescuing me."

"We're not out of here yet."

"What could possibly happen now?" Angel asked. "I mean—"

Angel was in his arms so fast, it was as though an unseen force had shoved her there. One of his hands fisted in her hair, the other held her hips hard against his. They were aligned from breast to belly, and there was no mistaking his arousal.

"Does that answer your question?" he de-manded.

"Of all the dim-witted—"

"Don't start," he warned. "I was doing just fine until you started all that touching. I had put every picture I had of you out of my mind and—"

"What pictures?"

"You backed up against a sheer rock wall, that white gold hair of yours flying in the wind. The way your breasts looked straining against that damned excuse for a shirt you're wearing. The sight of those blue eyes of yours flashing defiance against impossible odds. I haven't stopped wanting you since the first moment I laid eyes on you, lady. If you're smart, you won't provoke me into taking what you've got to offer."

"I should've known you were just like all the others," she hissed. "Texas Ranger, my eye. Where's your badge, Dallas? I had hold of your shirt pocket, and it wasn't there."

"I took it off."

"What for?"

"I'm on a leave of absence."

"Why?"

He hesitated, then said in a stark, quiet voice, "A friend of mine, another Texas Ranger, was killed three days ago saving my worthless hide."

"I'm sorry," Angel murmured.

His grasp tightened on her. "Sorry doesn't help, Angel. If I'd been the one who was killed, there was nobody to give a damn. Cale left a wife and two kids behind. And I lost a friend who was like a brother to me.

"I walked into this cave trying to figure out some reason why he's dead and I'm still alive.

Alive enough to want a woman. Alive enough to want you!''

"Dallas, I—"

It was too late for words. His lips found hers in the dark, and this time he wasn't gentle. The same mouth that had been so soft was hard with unrestrained need. Ravaging. Plundering. Taking instead of giving.

Behind the need Angel felt his anguish, and she responded to it. Her arms circled him in comfort. Her body softened against his, offering solace. As suddenly as it had begun, the desperation receded, leaving only the need.

He could easily have taken what he wanted from her. She couldn't have resisted him; he was much bigger, much stronger than she. But as reason returned, his mouth left hers. His arms surrounded her, and he lifted her off the ground as he hid his face in the fall of silky hair at her shoulder.

Angel felt the strain in his body as he fought his grief. He shuddered once, and she felt him swallow hard. She reached up a hand and smoothed his hair back from his brow.

"It's all right," she crooned. "It wasn't your fault. I know you must have done everything you could. Why, you rescued me today without a whisker of thought for your own safety."

He didn't answer her, but he didn't push her away, either. She murmured comforting words, words she knew would not bring back his friend, but which might make him believe his was not such a worthless hide, after all.

For the first time in her life Angel was grateful for the dark. It had allowed this stranger to seek her out; it had allowed her to comfort him. Yet neither had to face the other when he at last lowered her to the ground and stepped away from her.

"Thanks," he said.

"You're welcome."

Dallas took her hand again, and they began to walk. He kept close to the wall to maintain his bearings, until at last the darkness gave way to gray shadows.

"I can see light," Angel said.

Dallas began to move faster, but Angel wasn't about to be left behind now. They were almost running when he suddenly stopped.

There it was. The entrance to the cave. The sun was shining. The grass was bright green except where spring wildflowers left splashes of orange and yellow.

Angel's heart skipped a beat. *That was wrong.* There shouldn't be any spring flowers. It was fall. An unusually early frost had already turned the grass brown. But perhaps these were fall flowers;

and maybe the frost hadn't caught this particular glen.

She stayed beside Dallas as they left the cave. Bees buzzed. Birds sang. The mesquite blossomed.

Angel held tightly to Dallas's hand. "It's very pretty here."

"It's always like this in the spring."

Angel frowned and looked up at Dallas…and caught her breath when she saw his face in the light. How could he have called those eyes brown? They were hazel, dancing with flecks of green. His hair might have been brown once upon a time, but the sun had streaked it with chestnut and gold. His face wasn't handsome, nor was it plain. But the wide-set eyes, the cheekbones, the strong jaw were undeniably appealing. And the mouth…

"Don't look at me like that," Dallas said. "Not unless you're willing this time to finish what you start."

Angel's gaze left his mouth and met his eyes with their ridiculous curly lashes. "I know this has been a trying few hours. But did you just say that it's spring?"

"It is," he said.

"It's not," Angel contradicted.

His brow furrowed. He reached out and gently

brushed aside the hair that covered her bruised forehead. ''Are you all right?''

She brushed his hand away. ''When you carried me into the cave it was October.''

''It's April.''

''October,'' she argued.

He shook his head. ''No, Angel. I'm afraid not.''

''I don't understand.''

He thrust a hand through his sun-streaked hair. ''Maybe you blocked things out—the shock of being attacked and all,'' he suggested.

She shook her head. ''I remember everything that's happened to me since the minute those six cowboys cornered me against that rock.''

''Look, maybe I'd better get you to a doctor.''

''I don't need a doctor,'' Angel insisted. ''You do.''

''Yeah, well, maybe—''

Dallas had been urging Angel forward beyond the hills that framed the cave opening. As the terrain leveled, she stopped dead at the sight of something extraordinary in front of her. ''What's that?''

''What?''

She pointed. ''That thing. What is it?''

Dallas looked worried. ''Look, maybe you bumped your head in there worse than you thought.'' He reached out to the small lump on her forehead.

''No. I'm fine,'' she insisted. ''It's just a scratch.'' She stared at him expectantly, then looked over at the strange black object.

''You really don't know what that is?''

''No. I really don't. Do you?''

''It's my pickup truck.''

''So? What is it?''

Dallas stepped away and looked long and hard at her. ''If this is some kind of joke, it isn't funny.''

''Why would I joke about something like this?'' she demanded.

''Where have you been living? This is the twentieth century. Everyone knows—''

She grabbed his arm so tight her nails dug into his flesh. ''Did you say the *twentieth* century?''

''Yes. So?''

Angel swallowed hard. ''That isn't possible.''

''Why not?''

''Because it's 1864.''

This time it was Dallas's turn to stare. ''It's 1992.''

Angel shook her head in denial. ''You're wrong. When you dragged me into that cave, it was October 3, 1864,'' she insisted.

"When I stepped in from this side, it was April 14, 1992," Dallas countered.

Angel's eyes went wide as she backed away from him. "How could that be?"

"I don't know," Dallas said. His lips flattened into a thin line. "But if what you're saying is the truth—" he paused, and it was clear he wasn't sure whether to believe her or not "—there's sure as hell no going back the way you came. If you are from the past, it looks to me like you're trapped here with me—in the future."

Angel felt the sunlight dimming around her, forming a single tunnel of darkness. It sucked her down, like a whirlpool, and she felt herself surely, inexorably sliding into it.

2

Dallas had faced a loaded gun with calm, but when Angel fainted, he panicked. Somehow, in the time they had spent together in the cave, she had touched some inner part of him that had been held inviolate since his youth. When he saw her collapsing, it was as though something dear to him, something necessary to his very existence, was threatened. Adrenaline flowed, and with superhuman effort he leapt forward and caught her before she hit the ground. Unsure what had caused her to lose consciousness, terrified that she had hurt her head far worse than either of them had suspected, he lifted the slight weight of her limp body into his arms and held her close.

"Angel?"

As he stood staring down at her, he realized that he was in serious danger of stepping over some invisible boundary. He felt the threat. And the temptation.

He fought his inclination to succumb and managed to bring himself back to a more objective state of mind. She was just another victim he had rescued from the forces of evil, nothing more and nothing less. She meant nothing to him. No woman did. No woman ever would.

Still, he couldn't shake his concern when she didn't immediately regain consciousness. He quickly carried her to his pickup, and after one-handedly arranging a blanket, he lowered her onto the back seat of the extended cab of the truck. He smoothed the hair off her forehead, exposing a bruise.

When you dragged me into the cave it was 1864.

Either she was the best liar he'd ever met, or she'd hurt herself worse then either of them knew. It was impossible to think she had somehow crossed over a threshold from the past. Wasn't it?

Right now he had to get her to a doctor as quickly as possible. As he slid behind the wheel and headed the pickup toward San Antonio, he realized he was in something of a dilemma. No doctor was going to believe Angel if she told him she was from the past. Most likely she'd end up committed to some mental institution. And if the doctor did believe her? She'd end up under a microscope in some top-secret government laboratory.

The possibility that Angel had come from the

past seemed slight to nonexistent. The only thing in her favor was the quaint language she used. It had been in evidence long before there had been any discussion of where—or when—she had come from.

Unfortunately the cowboys who had surrounded Angel hadn't looked much different from cowboys today. It was unusual that they'd been on horseback, but not entirely unlikely even in this day and age. Dallas tried to remember distinguishing features about the men who had held Angel at bay. It was hard because once he had caught sight of Angel, he hadn't been able to drag his eyes off her.

Then he realized that there had been an usual yellow stripe down the outside seam of two of the men's trousers. Gray trousers. *Confederate* trousers? His memory must be playing tricks on him. He realized that he wanted to believe her, because he didn't want to contemplate the fact that she was really hurt or crazy.

It was too bad Angel had lost the rucksack he had seen her set down outside the cave. Maybe there would have been something in it either to prove or disprove her claim. Dallas hadn't thought to check the pockets of her trousers, but he would have her do that—or do it himself—as soon as he got her home.

Home.

Dallas shoved a hand through his hair in agitation. Where had the idea come from to take her home with him instead of directly to San Antonio? He had no business even considering it. He made the turn to take him west to his ranch on the Frio River outside Uvalde, even as he told himself it was a dumb thing to do.

"Where am I?"

Dallas looked over his shoulder and felt relieved to see Angel sitting up.

"You're in the back of my pickup—my truck," he explained when she looked confused.

She winced as her fingertips found the wound on her forehead. "I wasn't dreaming?"

He shook his head ruefully. "I'm afraid not, Angel."

Angel's attention had been focused on the man; now it shifted to her surroundings. Her jaw dropped in amazement. She swallowed hard and said, "We're moving awfully fast."

"No more than sixty miles an hour."

"That isn't possible! What's making this… truck…go?"

"Nowadays the horses are under the hood," Dallas said with a wry smile. He caught a glimpse of Angel's horrified expression in the mirror. This was no time for an explanation of the internal combustion engine, so he said, "A mechanical contraption inside the front of the truck makes it go."

Angel waved a hand at all the dials and knobs in front of him. "What do all those buttons do?"

Dallas punched a knob and a country and western tune started playing. "Radio," he said.

Fascinated, Angel asked, "How does it work?"

"Don't ask me," Dallas said, shaking his head. "I don't understand the innards of most of the modern conveniences I use."

He punched another button and a blast of cool air hit Angel in the face.

"Air-conditioning," he explained.

Another button made windshield wipers scrape across the bug-spattered glass; yet another sent water spraying up to clean off the bugs.

"Things have certainly changed a lot," Angel said, in perhaps the understatement of the century.

"Lady, you don't know the half of it. Why, we can fly across the entire country in a couple of hours."

Angel's cheeks flushed with anger. "Now you're making fun of me. We both know men can't fly."

"Men can't. Airplanes can."

"Airplanes?"

"Another mechanical contraption, like a truck with wings, only it moves in the air."

"I don't believe you."

"It's the truth, whether you believe me or not. Stay around long enough and I'll show you one. Hell, I'll even take you up in one!"

"No, thanks," Angel said vehemently.

"Whether you can accept it or not, there's been a lot of progress in the past hundred and twenty-five or so years."

"The clothes you're wearing are the same," she protested.

Dallas looked down at the chambray shirt, jeans, and boots he was wearing. "Maybe men's fashions haven't changed much. But women show a lot more skin than they used to. Come to think of it, that outfit you're wearing doesn't fit my image of what a woman in 1864 ought to have on.

"In *Gone with the Wind* Scarlett O'Hara was wearing something a little more feminine than that getup, as I recall."

Angel wondered who Scarlett O'Hara was. She fingered the top button of the striped cotton, round-necked man's shirt, its sleeves folded up to reveal her slender forearms. A hemp rope held up the too-large, patched wool trousers. On her feet she wore knee-high black boots. "I was traveling dressed as a man, so I wouldn't be harassed on the road,'' she explained.

Dallas glanced at the silvery blond hair that fell practically to her waist and said, ''You're not going to fool too many men with hair like that.''

''My hair was tucked up under a farmer's hat. I had it off because I'd stopped for a drink of water at that pond near the cave opening. That's when those piss-poor excuses for cowboys rode up and—'' She shrugged. ''You know the rest.''

''I guess the question now is, what am I going to do with you?'' Dallas murmured to himself.

Angel bristled. ''You don't have to do anything with me. I can take care of myself.''

Dallas drove through a gate and across a cattle guard that led onto his property. ''Maybe in 1864 you could have managed by yourself—although even that's doubtful, considering the situation I found you in. Here in 1992, you're as naive as a newborn. You wouldn't last ten seconds on your own.'' Dallas pursed his lips in disgust. ''I guess I'm stuck with you, all right.''

''Stuck with me! Why of all the cabbage-headed, tom-doodle ideas I ever heard—''

Dallas hit the brakes and the truck fishtailed on gravel as it skidded to a stop. He half turned in the seat and grabbed Angel by the shoulders, drawing her toward him until they were nose to nose.

"Look, you—you nincompoop," he flung at her, having searched for and found a word as quaint as any of hers. "I'm not any happier about this situation than you are. But let's get one thing straight. I'm not a cabbage head, a tom-doodle or any of the other names you've called me since we had the misfortune to meet. In some convoluted way, I suppose I'm to blame for your predicament."

"I'll say!" Angel snapped.

He glared at her and continued, "I've never shirked my responsibilities, and I don't intend to start now. I'll be by your side every second until I think you're capable of surviving in this century. Have you got that?"

He shoved her back into the seat, let go and stared at her, daring her to move.

If he'd known Angel better, he wouldn't have thrown down the gauntlet quite so dramatically. As it was, she was nose to nose with him again in a matter of seconds.

"Now *you* listen to *me*," Angel said, punctuating her speech with a finger poking at his chest. "I've been on my own since I was fourteen. And I travel alone—when I please and where I please. Is *that* clear?"

"As a pane of glass," he said. "But it doesn't change a thing. Until I say different, you travel with me, and you go where I say." He didn't give her a chance to argue, just turned back to the wheel, started the engine and peeled out so she was slung back against the seat by the force of the truck's acceleration.

Angel stared at the swiftly passing landscape—bone-dry rolling prairie dotted with mesquite and cactus—and realized she had just missed her best chance to escape from this madman before they arrived at wherever he was taking her. She felt trapped, and she didn't like it. But Angel had spent her life making the best of bad situations. This was no different. At least that's what she tried to tell herself.

"Does your insistence on keeping me with you mean that you believe I'm from the past?" Angel asked.

"I don't know what to believe," Dallas admitted. "But until I'm sure one way or the other, I don't intend to take any chances with you."

"Why should you care what happens to me?"

"I'm a lawman. It's my duty to help the helpless."

"You told me yourself you're on a leave of absence from duty," Angel countered. "And besides, I'm far from helpless."

"Then chalk it up to the Code of the West," Dallas said. "A man protects a woman. That's just the way things are done—even today. By the way, have you got anything on you that could *prove* you're from the past?"

Angel touched her pants pocket protectively. The paper was still there. "No. Nothing." *Nothing I want to show you.*

Dallas stopped the truck in front of a peak-roofed two-story white frame house. Several moss-draped live oaks shaded the house, which had a covered porch that ran across the front of it. Victorian gingerbread trim decorated the porch and the eaves. Old-fashioned forest-green shutters flanked the front windows, upstairs and down. It was not a twentieth century house—at least not on the outside.

Dallas stepped out of the truck and helped Angel down. He held on to her hand as he led her up the front porch steps and into the house. He told himself it was because she might need his support. The truth was he felt an unusual sense of possessiveness that made him never want to let her go. He labeled it a delayed reaction to saving her life and tried not to think about it.

Angel stared at the room, which was a mixture of both strange and recognizable objects. "Do you live here alone?"

"I have since my father was shot and killed ten years ago."

"I'm sorry." She turned and her blue eyes met his hazel ones, full of sympathy and understanding. "Indians? Or outlaws?"

Dallas stared at her for a moment. That was the sort of instinctual response that could only be made by someone to whom marauding Comanches were still a threat. Someone from the past. "Outlaws," he said at last. "My father also was a Texas Ranger. He was shot trying to save a child who'd been kidnapped."

By now Angel had touched almost everything in the room with which she was familiar—the Victorian sofa, the pine trestle table and four chairs, the sideboard, the standing hat rack, the shelves full of leather-bound books and the mantel over the stone fireplace. She had avoided everything else.

Dallas picked up a black object and punched buttons on it. "Hi, Doc," he said into one end of the object. "I wondered if you could make a house call. I don't know if you'd call it an emergency. More like a necessary visit. I can't explain on the phone. Good. I'll be here."

"What is that you're holding?" Angel asked. "Why were you speaking into it?"

"It's a phone. It's used to talk to people who are somewhere else."

Angel frowned. "Magic?"

"No. It's mechanical. Although I don't know if you'd call fiber optics exactly mechanical," Dallas said with a humorous twist of his lips. "Maybe magic *is* the better word."

"How does it work?"

Dallas grimaced. Every question she asked pointed out his ignorance of the technical world in which he lived. "I just know how to work it, not how it works," he admitted. "The world's not a simple place anymore. There's a lot we accept on faith. Like, if I turn on the stove I get heat. The refrigerator keeps things cold. I turn a spigot and water comes out, punch a button and the television works. These days people learn specific jobs and don't know much beyond their own particular skill."

"Sort of like the butcher and the baker and the blacksmith each has a trade?" Angel asked.

"Exactly the same," he agreed. "Only things have gotten a lot more complicated since computers were invented."

Angel didn't understand a tenth of what Dallas was saying. The words he used meant nothing, provoked no images of anything with which she was familiar. It was hard not to feel overwhelmed.

And frightened. Much as she hated to admit it, perhaps staying with Dallas wasn't such a bad idea—at least until she could absorb and understand some of the shocking changes the world had undergone. Or until she could figure out some way to get back to her life in the past.

"Would you like to see the rest of the house?" Dallas asked.

"I suppose."

Dallas showed Angel the kitchen, demonstrating modern appliances that kept her eyebrows perpetually raised in astonishment. The bathroom had a sink, toilet and tub, all of which she longed to use. There were three bedrooms. The two bedrooms upstairs were filled with furniture he called antiques, but which she found achingly familiar. The downstairs bedroom had been converted into an office. Besides what Dallas described as "a bed hidden in the sofa," the room contained more mechanical devices, including a mystical "computer" that had apparently revolutionized the way things were done in the modern world.

"Would it be all right if I take a bath?" Angel asked, looking longingly in the direction of the large indoor tub she had seen.

Dallas frowned. "I'd feel better if Doc Philips checked you out before I leave you alone behind a closed door."

"How long before he gets here?"

A knock on the door answered her question. "I suspect that's him now."

Dallas opened the door to a handsome young man, not much older than he, wearing a white Oxford cloth shirt and jeans with a denim jacket. His eyes were a startling blue and openly curious when he spotted Angel.

Dallas put a protective arm around Angel's shoulders and pulled her forward. "Angel, this is Dr. Adam Philips. We grew up as neighbors. Adam, this is Angel Taylor."

"You both look pretty healthy to me," Adam said. "Why the urgent call?"

Dallas's gaze slid to Angel and back to the doctor. "Everything isn't always what it seems."

"Meaning?"

"Angel has a bump on her head. I'd like you to check it out."

Dallas met Adam's questioning gaze but shook his head slightly to indicate he didn't want to talk.

"All right," Adam said. "Let's get to it. How about if you lie down on the couch, Angel, and I'll look you over."

Angel eyed the doctor's black bag anxiously. She had never had much use for doctors. She tensed as he pulled a small object out of the bag.

He pushed a button and the contraption in his hand lit up. She sat up abruptly. "What's that?"

Adam looked at her and then at Dallas before he answered. "A sort of flashlight, so I can see into your eyes."

"What's a flashlight?" Angel demanded suspiciously.

Dallas saw in Adam's expression the concern about Angel that he had been feeling himself for the past several hours. He listened as Adam calmly explained the inner mechanism of a flashlight, down to how a battery worked, and found himself chagrined to be learning along with Angel. All the time Adam talked, the doctor slowly but thoroughly examined his patient.

Angel was relieved when the doctor took an ordinary stethoscope from his bag, but became concerned again when he withdrew what he said was a blood-pressure cuff. He was straightforward in his explanations of everything he did before he did it, answering her questions as though they weren't at all unusual. Though his instruments frightened her, nothing he did in his examination hurt her. He cleaned her skinned knee using something from a unique spraying can, then covered it with gauze and tape.

When Adam had finished with his medical examination, he stood up and walked over to talk privately with Dallas. "The skinned knee is superficial. As far as I can tell, the bump on her head is just that—a bump. There's no sign of concussion. Or anything else I can find to explain why she doesn't seem to recognize some very ordinary objects when they're presented to her. That is why you called me, isn't it? There's something wrong with her memory. Some kind of selective amnesia?"

"Not exactly," Dallas hedged.

"If that's all you're going to say, I can't be any more help to you." Adam headed for the door, medical bag in hand.

Dallas caught up to his friend on the porch. "I can't tell you any more right now."

"Fine," Adam said and kept walking.

Dallas let Adam get into his car before he finally came striding after him. He leaned down so he could see in the window of the low-slung sports car. "Do you think Angel is crazy?" he blurted.

"What do you mean? Clinically nuts?"

Dallas nodded curtly.

Adam brushed his thumbs across the black leather cover on the steering wheel. "That's hard to say without a psychological examination. Do you think she's crazy?"

"I don't know what to think."

"To tell you the truth, I was more than a little surprised to find a woman—any woman—in your house. I didn't think you brought them here."

"I don't," Dallas said flatly. "Angel is different."

"Where did you find her?"

"I rescued her from some cowboys who were giving her a hard time."

"At least that's in character for you. Look," Adam offered, "I can set up an appointment for Angel with a psychiatrist, if you like."

"Not right now," Dallas said. "Maybe later."

"Are you going to tell me what this is all about?"

"I'll explain everything later," Dallas promised. He stroked the sleek finish of the sports car. "Don't fall into any potholes with this baby car of yours on the way out."

Adam grinned. "You're just jealous. Call me if you need me."

"Sure."

Dallas stood and watched until the dust settled, before he turned and walked back into the house. Angel was no longer lying on the sofa where he'd left her.

"Angel? Where are you?"

There was no response.

Dallas quickly began a search of the house, going from room to room, slamming open doors, checking into closets and finding nothing.

At last he approached the bathroom and shoved open the door. There she stood, staring at him with startled blue eyes.

His breath caught in his chest. His heart skipped a beat. His mouth suddenly went dry.

She was wearing a different sort of underwear. The camisole top had been loosened where it laced up the front, and he could see the creamy swell of her breasts through the white laces. He watched a bead of water slide down her skin and dampen the cotton.

Below the waist she was wearing some kind of loose knee-length pants that were strictly puritanical. She quickly crossed one arm over her breasts and the other over the delta between her thighs. But it was far too late to keep his imagination from running wild.

"Why didn't you answer me?" he rasped.

"I didn't hear you. The water was running. I just wanted—needed—to rinse off some of the dust."

"Go ahead," he said. But instead of leaving, he stood there, staring at her.

Angel had seen that kind of hunger in a man's eyes in the past, but never before had she felt compelled to appease it. She wasn't sure exactly

what was happening to her. It was as though she
were caught in another kind of time warp, one
where each moment was held suspended, giving
her the time to identify each and every thrilling
sensation as it occurred. And equal time to become aware of Dallas's avid response to her slow
but steady arousal.

Her breasts felt full and achy.

*His eyes lowered and his gaze caused her nip-
ples to harden.*

Her mouth felt dry. It was hard to swallow.

*His lips parted slightly, to ease breathing that
had become harsh to the ear.*

She pressed her thighs together, to hold on to
the warmth and wetness that had mysteriously appeared between her legs.

*His nostrils flared for the scent of her. A muscle
worked in his jaw as he clenched his teeth.*

She felt her body arching toward him, thrusting
breasts and hips forward in a way that begged him
to touch.

*His lids lowered over lambent eyes. His body
tensed, muscles tautening with barely restrained
need.*

Dallas was a man who appreciated beautiful
women. But never had he wanted a woman as
much as he wanted Angel. His hand reached out

and cupped her breast, and he had the satisfaction of hearing a groan of pleasure deep in her throat.

His thumb brushed across her nipple, creating a vivid peak beneath the cloth. "I can't believe this is really happening," he murmured. "What force of nature brought you here?"

Angel came to her senses and took a step back. When Dallas started to reach for her again she warned, "I wouldn't do that if I were you. I've had to defend myself from forward men once or twice in the past. You wouldn't escape unscathed."

Dallas throbbed, he was so aroused. But the hellion before him had made it plain he would be lucky to escape with his life if he tried touching her again.

"It seems a tease is still a tease whatever century she comes from," he accused.

Angel had pushed reality away for a moment, but now it was back with a vengeance. Before her stood a very angry, very frustrated man. "I'm not a tease! I came in here *alone* to rinse off some of the trail dust. If you'll recall, you're the one who came barging in unannounced."

"You didn't send me away," he pointed out.

"You're right. That was a mistake I won't make again. I'll have your apology and you can go," she said.

He swore under his breath. "When hell freezes over."

They were at a stalemate.

It was plain from the look on Dallas's face that he didn't believe Angel was innocent of purposefully trying to entice him. But it was the truth. Angel had no explanation for her unusual behavior. Exactly what *had* happened, anyway? Was it possible the Texas Ranger had cast some sort of spell over her? Had something been invented in the twentieth century to aid in the seduction of innocent virgins? She shuddered at the thought.

"You're cold," Dallas said, misinterpreting her reaction. He reached to grab a man-sized towel from the nearby rack, and she stepped back until she hit the tile wall. It wasn't nearly far enough.

"Keep your distance, Ranger, and we'll get along fine."

A flash of irritation crossed his face. "I only thought you might want to dry off a little," he said, extending the towel at arm's length.

"Thank you," she said, taking it from him with exaggerated dignity. "You may leave now."

Dallas had already turned his back when he realized that she had dismissed him. Perversely he wasn't about to let her have the last word. He stuck out his hand to catch the door before she could shut it in his face.

"I like that mole on your right breast," he said.

Angel gasped. "You clunch! How dare you—"

"One day I'll wash it myself. With my tongue."

He let go, and the door slammed in his face. Dallas grinned as he listened to the unique imprecations she muttered behind the door. She was stubborn, all right, and opinionated. She also had gumption. That didn't mean he was going to take any more guff from her. He was responsible for her, and by God she was going to do as she was told!

Angel leaned her forehead against the door, fistfuls of the towel clutched against her bosom. What an impossible man! How could he have mentioned something so personal? She couldn't stand him! He was horrible! Dealing with him was like being up the same tree as a grizzly. How could she be so attracted to someone so intolerable?

She sighed and turned to look at herself in the mirror. The problem was, sparks flew whenever she got near him. That was going to have to stop. She wasn't sure how she'd been propelled into the future. But she had business that needed finishing in the past.

Angel reached down and pulled a paper out of the pocket of her trousers. She unfolded it and looked at the image printed there. Across the top of the paper was the caption WANTED. She stared at it for another moment, her lips flattened in a bitter line. Then she folded the poster and put it away again. Likely the Ranger wouldn't approve if he found out where she had been heading. But what Dallas Masterson didn't know wouldn't hurt him.

She twisted the knobs on the tub the way Dallas had shown her. As long as she was in the future, she might as well take advantage of the opportunity to get a hot indoor bath. Sometime soon she was going to have to go back where she had come from.

3
___

Dallas paced the floor of the living room most of the night, trying to decide what he should do next. The several times he checked on Angel, she was sleeping like a baby in his bed. It was easy to see how serene she was, because she had asked to keep the bedside lamp on. He wondered why she was so afraid of the dark and whether there was any way to help her get over her fear. The fact he was so concerned worried him. It wasn't a smart move to get any more involved with her than he already was.

Unfortunately, knowing the smart move and making it were two entirely different things.

When Dallas awoke in the morning, he was draped half on and half off the Victorian sofa. Someone—it must have been Angel—had thrown the quilt from his bed over him. The smell of perking coffee permeated the room. He slowly sat up, stretching kinks out of knotted muscles as he went.

"Oh. I didn't know you were awake. I borrowed some of your clothes. I hope you don't mind.''

"Not at all.''

Angel stood before him wearing a western shirt from his closet and a clean pair of his jeans, folded up at the ankle and tied with the same rope he'd seen around her waist the previous day. Her hair fell over her shoulders practically to her waist. She looked more fragile this morning, dressed in his oversize clothes. The feeling of protectiveness arose even stronger than before. He ignored it and focused on the coffee cup she held in her hands. "I see you figured out how to work the stove.''

She grinned. "It sure beats gathering kindling for a fire. The coffeepot was on a back burner, and I found the coffee grounds by opening cupboards and sniffing. Would you like this cup? I can get myself another.''

"That's all right. I can get a cup for myself.''

Before he could stand, she laid a hand on his bare chest. "Don't get up.''

Dallas couldn't have moved if his life depended on it. Even though she was barely touching him, he was distinctly aware of her fingertips on his flesh.

Angel was amazed at how hot his skin felt. She was intimately aware of the crisp hair under her fingers, of the firm muscle that tensed beneath her touch. She withdrew her hand ever so slowly, as though she were escaping a trap that might spring closed if she weren't extremely careful.

She set the coffee cup on the low wooden table beside the sofa, said ''I'll be right back'' and turned to go.

Dallas stood and caught her wrist before she had gone two steps. ''Don't leave.''

Angel glanced over her shoulder and froze at the sight of him. The hair on his chest arrowed toward his belly. Her eyes followed the dark line down until it was cut off by his jeans. The top button was undone, and they had slid down his hips. Beneath the worn blue denim was the unmistakable proof that he was as aware of her as she was of him.

Angel didn't resist his hold on her wrist, merely poised herself to flee or fight, whichever alternative should offer her the best chance of survival.

Only, to her surprise, Dallas released her.

''I didn't mean to frighten you,'' he said.

''You didn't,'' Angel lied. She saw him wince as she rubbed her wrist where he had held her.

''Did I hurt you?''

''No.'' He hadn't, she realized. But she could still feel his flesh on hers. The sensation had been stunning.

They weren't touching now, but an invisible bond seemed to hold them in thrall. Neither moved, neither broke the spell until finally Angel realized that she was waiting for him to make the first move, to touch her again. That wasn't fair to him…or to her. She had gone her whole life without being touched by a man as much as Dallas had touched her in the past twenty-four hours. It was foolish to get embroiled in something she wouldn't be around to finish.

"Can I—" She had to stop and clear her throat before she could continue. "Can I make you some breakfast?"

Dallas smiled. Trust a woman to think of a man's stomach at a time like this. "A couple of fried eggs and some bacon would be fine," he said. "I'll come along and show you where things are."

Angel hesitated and then nodded.

Once they had something to do, it wasn't so hard being in the same room with each other. The tension was always there, but they could channel it into action and thus defuse it.

Angel found the contents of the refrigerator a marvel. Imagine the convenience of a dozen eggs in a plastic carton and bacon already sliced and ready to fry! She laughed when Dallas showed her the pre-made biscuits in a cardboard cylinder. They weren't half-bad.

Dallas didn't say much while they ate, but it wasn't a peaceful silence. Angel knew he was agitated. He opened his mouth several times to speak, then snapped it shut again. She didn't press him. In her experience it was best to let a man do his thinking without interruption. When he was ready, he would talk.

Only, when Dallas finally spoke she wasn't at all pleased with what he had to say.

"I made a mistake bringing you here, Angel. I should have taken you to San Antonio, to a hospital or somewhere they can take care of you."

"You don't believe me," she said flatly. "I mean, that I'm from the past."

His eyes were bleak. "No, I don't."

"Then take me back to the cave," Angel said.

He shook his head. "That wouldn't solve anything. The tunnel's gone. If—and it's a big if—you did come from the past, there's no going back."

"There must be another way, another tunnel. I have to get back where I came from," Angel said, her voice strained with the effort to remain calm. "There's someone—"

"You said you don't have any family," Dallas interrupted.

"It's not— You don't understand."

"Then explain it to me."

Angel took one look at the implacable man sitting across from her and realized he wasn't going anywhere until she talked. "All I can say is that I have business, unfinished *personal* business, that needs tending to in San Antonio. In the past."

Dallas wondered whether her personal business involved another man. He felt a stab of jealousy at the thought. "Anything you can share?"

"Believe me, I'd tell you everything if I thought it would make a difference," she said. "But there's nothing you can do to help—except get me back to the past."

Dallas scratched the dark beard on his jaw. He really ought to shave. With that thought came the memory of why he hadn't shaved, why he had been in the cave in the first place. He realized that somehow his guilt over Cale's death had eased. Angel had done that for him in the darkness of the cave. So maybe he owed her the chance to prove to him that she was from the past, and perhaps to help her find her way back to wherever she came from.

"All right," he said. "We'll go back to the cave. We'll look for another exit. But if we don't find it—"

"We'll find it," Angel said. "We have to."

"And if we don't?"

The air in Angel's lungs hissed out, but she managed a tremulous smile. "Then I guess you're stuck with me."

Dallas liked that idea too much to spend time contemplating it.

They didn't say anything more, just finished the food on their plates. Angel offered to wash the dishes before they left for the cave, but Dallas grinned and opened a door under the sink. "Automatic dishwasher. All you have to do is stack the dishes inside and the machine does the rest."

"Now that's something almost worth staying in the future to have," Angel said. *"Almost,"* she repeated, when it looked like Dallas was going to suggest she do just that.

The drive back to the cave was no less harrowing in Angel's eyes. She couldn't get used to the speed of Dallas's truck. Somehow everything in the future seemed geared to happen in a hurry. It was like landing on a bucking bronc. She wanted off. She wanted things to slow down, so she could breathe easily again.

"I lost most of my gear in the cave-in, so all I've got is a couple of flashlights," Dallas said. "We'll stay together. At least you won't have to worry about the dark. There's only one other tunnel I haven't followed, and that's because it starts wet and stays that way.''

"Wet?''

"An underground river runs through the tunnel. It's shallow—what I've seen of it. That doesn't mean it doesn't get deeper. Or end up going underground.''

Dallas didn't believe they would come out of the cave in another century, but he wasn't taking any chances. He carried all the usual cavers' supplies—and brought along his gun. He carried the same .45 Colt revolver his father and his father's father had carried, rather than the automatic weapon the department issued.

"Expecting trouble?'' Angel asked as he slipped the gun into a holster at his side.

"Never hurts to be prepared,'' he said.

The way back through the cave didn't seem to take nearly so long with flashlights. Dallas took Angel directly to the spot where the cave had come crashing down behind them.

"There's no going back that way,'' he confirmed. "But over there—'' he shifted his flashlight to expose another opening in the rock "—that's the other tunnel I mentioned to you.''

Angel hadn't noticed the sound of running water before, but it was clear to her now. "Do you have any suggestions how we do this?''

"I go first. You follow me. I decide whether we keep going or turn back."

"All right. Let's go."

Dallas hadn't expected her to agree so readily, but he was glad she hadn't argued. He had enough bad feelings about doing this. He didn't like the idea of heading into the dark in ankle-deep water with nothing more than a couple of flashlights to show the way.

The water was cold, but it stayed shallow for the first half hour. There was a slight current, but hardly enough to cause a ripple. Angel was nervous; the flashlights didn't provide quite enough light to make her comfortable in the dark. She eased her fear by talking, asking Dallas questions.

"Why did you become a Texas Ranger?"

"The men in my family have been lawmen for generations."

"What if you'd wanted to do something else?"

"I didn't."

"What happened to your mother?"

"She just up and left one day."

"How awful for you. How old were you when it happened?"

"Seventeen."

"Why did she leave?"

"Don't you ever get tired of asking questions?" Dallas asked in exasperation.

"No. Why did she leave?"

"You'd have to ask her that."

"Belinda and I were just kids, babies almost, when we ended up in an orphanage and—"

"Who's Belinda?"

"Belinda is—" Angel swallowed hard "—she was my sister."

Dallas stopped and turned back to shine his flashlight on Angel's face. Her features looked grim in the stark light. "I thought you said you didn't have any family."

"I don't. Belinda's dead. She was shot."

"Shot!"

"There was a bank robbery in San Antonio a week ago. She happened to be in the wrong place at the wrong time." Angel tried shrugging away the tremendous anger she felt at the injustice of it all. For Belinda to have survived everything they had lived through during the war, only to be killed in a bank robbery, seemed a cruel fate.

"Does her death have anything to do with why you were on your way to San Antonio?" Dallas asked.

"What if it does?"

"Her funeral?"

"Too late for that."

"What then?" Dallas asked.

"It's none of your business."

Dallas stared at Angel. The hard set of her jaw, the fierce look in her blue eyes, made him want to shake the truth out of her. She was heading into trouble. He knew it as sure as he knew cactus had thorns.

He turned and started away again, moving fast, causing Angel to have to run to keep up with him.

"Slow down," she cried. "I—"

All of a sudden Dallas stopped and turned and caught hold of her arms. "There was no bank robbery in San Antonio a week ago," he said.

"Maybe not in 1992," she said bitterly. "There was in 1864."

"Why don't you give up this make-believe—"

"It's not pretend! It's real!" Angel retorted in frustration. "I know it sounds farfetched. I wouldn't believe it myself, except I can't argue with these—these gadgets of yours." She waved the flashlight at him. "You don't have to believe me. Just get me back where I was. That's all I ask. The rest will take care of itself."

"And if you can't get back?"

"I'd rather wait to worry about that until I have to," she said.

"Trouble. Nothing but trouble," Dallas muttered.

Angel arched a brow. "Look who's talking."

He turned on his heel and stalked off. She followed him. He walked slower, at least slow enough that she didn't have to run. But the water got deeper, first to Angel's calves, then to her knees.

"Let me know if you start to get chilled," Dallas said.

"I'm fine."

"If this gets any deeper, I think we'll have to turn back. I—"

Angel saw the light at the same time Dallas did. "There's an opening up there," she said.

"It appears so," he replied. "Be careful. Don't get in a hurry. That's how accidents happen."

Angel crowded him, but he refused to go any faster. He wasn't at all sure what he would find out there. Not that he believed it was going to be 1864, but who was to say whether those cowboys might not still be hanging around.

"Wait here," he said with they reached the opening. "I'll go first and make sure it's safe."

Dallas had been a lawman for a long time. He moved slowly and easily on his feet. His eyes narrowed as he searched the terrain. He listened. All his senses were attuned to any sign of movement. There was no threat to either of them that he could discern.

"All right. Come on out," he called to Angel.

Angel's heart was pounding as she stepped

over the darkened threshold into the light. She caught her breath when she saw the landscape. It didn't look familiar. But it didn't look strange, either. "I can't tell whether it's 1864, or not. Can you?"

Dallas was edgy. As much as he told himself he didn't believe Angel could have been telling the truth, he didn't like the look of the terrain. He told himself there weren't any spring flowers here because there wasn't as much shade on this side of the hill. He told himself the grass was probably dry because it hadn't gotten as much rain. Everyone in Texas knew the weather was so fickle it could rain on one side of a road and not the other. But he didn't like it.

"Any suggestions?" Dallas asked.

"We could start walking," Angel said, "until we come upon something that tells us for sure where we are. I mean, whether it's 1992 or 1864."

"I don't know, Angel. What if—" He'd been about to say, "What if we *are* in the past? I don't want to get stuck here." But he had told her time and again he didn't believe her story. So what was there to be afraid of? He could surely retrace their trail and find his way back here again. "All right," he agreed. "We'll walk."

This time it was Dallas who asked the questions.

"What would a woman like you do for a living...back then?"

Angel shrugged. "Most women I knew took care of their husbands and kids."

"But you never married?"

"No."

"Why not?"

"There was a boy I loved, but..." Angel felt the heaviness of heart that arose whenever she thought of Stephen. "He was killed last summer at the Battle of Gettysburg."

"Is that the *Civil War* you're talking about?" Dallas asked incredulously.

Angel nodded. "There isn't much honest work for a single woman during a war. But I managed."

"Are you suggesting you did *dishonest* work?"

Angel eyed him cautiously. "I might have stolen a steer or two."

"You were a *cattle rustler?*"

"Most recently."

"What did you do before that?" Dallas asked, almost afraid to hear her answer.

"Picked a few pockets in El Paso, played some poker with marked cards in saloons in Galveston.

Mostly I stayed out of the way of the war." She paused a moment and asked, "Who won?"

"The North."

She clucked her tongue. "It figures. All the signs were there. Did the Union take the South back?"

"It did. And grew some. There are fifty states now." But he didn't want to talk about the Civil War. He had more important things he wanted to know. "Are you planning to go back to the outlaw life?"

She shrugged. "Not much opportunity for a woman alone to make an honest living." Her features hardened. "And I'd rather steal than make a living on my back."

Dallas stopped in the small circle of shade provided by a mesquite and turned to confront Angel. "Why on earth do you want to go back if the life is so hard? Why not stay here in the future?"

"Is it any better for a woman in 1992?"

"A woman can do most anything a man can nowadays."

"Are there any woman Texas Rangers?" she asked.

"No," Dallas admitted. "But there are plenty of women police officers. Why you can—" Dallas stopped. He couldn't imagine what career to suggest for a woman who had been a cattle rustler, a pickpocket and a cardsharp. He didn't even know if Angel could read and write. "I'm sure there's something you could do," he muttered.

"What, exactly, did you have in mind?" Angel asked, her lips curling sardonically. "I don't understand even the simplest of your machines. What skill do I have that could possibly be translated into an honest profession in your world?"

"I don't know...yet." Dallas pulled off his Stetson, wiped his forehead with his bandanna, then settled his hat back low on his brow. "There's bound to be something honest you can do."

Angel snorted inelegantly. "You don't sound confident about that."

Dallas was worried. Not that he let Angel see what he was thinking. She obviously wasn't a hardened criminal, but with the road she was traveling, it wouldn't take but a few wrong turns and she'd end up spending her life in jail. He didn't know why he thought he could help her go straight. But from everything she said it sounded like she hadn't had too many breaks in the past. With some honest employment—

"I hear something," Angel said.

Dallas listened. "That droning sound?"

"Yes. Sounds sort of like bees or—"

"It's an airplane," Dallas said. He looked up

and when he spotted it, pointed. "Look there. See that? Where the sun is glinting off silver? That's an airplane. It looks like we're not in the past after all, Angel. I'm sorry."

"No, you're not," Angel said bitterly. "You're glad. Now you can believe I'm crazy or lying or whatever you want. And there's nothing I can do to prove differently."

Tears glittered in Angel's eyes.

"Angel? Are you all right?"

Her chin came up and her eyes flashed dangerously. She might be temporarily down, but she most certainly was not done in. "Of all the bean-headed—no, I'm not all right," she retorted. "I'm trapped in the future with a man who doesn't believe I'm from the past. I haven't any skills to make my way honestly, and that same man also just happens to be a Texas Ranger. No, I'd say I'm definitely *not* all right."

Dallas knew enough to keep his distance from a spitting wildcat. He offered verbal comfort instead. "Things aren't as bad as you think, Angel," he said. "I meant what I said. I'll help you find a job. You can stay with me until you find something you like, something you can do well."

Where had the inclination to make that offer come from? Dallas had lived alone since his father's death. He'd had only one use for women since his mother had walked out. Angel was clearly off limits for that purpose. She had made it plain her virtue was intact—and would stay that way. So why this sentimental reaction to a woman who was nothing more than a common thief? He had to be a little crazy himself.

Insane or not, he couldn't let her go. ''Come on, Angel,'' he coaxed. ''Say yes.''

She wanted to run away, but there was nowhere she could go. She wiped her stinging eyes on the sleeve of her shirt. So be it. She had fallen on hard times before. She had learned to take the bitter with the better. Any hopes of a ''normal'' life had been denied when her mother had put her and Belinda in the orphanage. Since then she'd had to struggle tooth and claw simply to survive.

Angel wished she had been able to make it to San Antonio. She had wanted the satisfaction of being there when... Better not to ponder what couldn't be changed. If she couldn't get back, she couldn't get back.

Only, Angel had serious qualms about the honest life the Ranger was offering her. She was willing to try it, but if it didn't work out... She had been taking care of herself a long time. She would manage somehow to take care of herself now, too.

''All right,'' Angel said. ''I'll go with you. But

I'll stay only until I learn what I need to know to survive on my own.''

"And get an honest job," Dallas added.

Angel lifted a brow. She didn't contradict him, just turned and headed back toward the cave opening.

"Look, Angel," Dallas said, marching along beside her. "This isn't really negotiable. I'm responsible for you. If you don't go along with me, I'll have to arrest you."

"For what? I haven't done anything illegal—in this century."

She had him there, all right. "We'll compromise," he said. "You cooperate with me and—"

Angel stopped at the cave entrance and turned to confront him, silvery hair flying in the wind. "I need your help," she conceded, "so I'll do what I can to get along with you. So long as you don't overstep your bounds."

"What bounds?" he asked, although he had a pretty good idea what she meant.

"Just keep your distance, Ranger."

"What are you afraid of, Angel? I wouldn't take anything you didn't offer."

That was the problem, Angel thought. He was the smoothest talking devil she'd ever met. When he touched her—well, firecrackers on the Fourth of July didn't make much more of an explosion.

"It's a hard world out there, Ranger. I have enough trouble taking care of myself. I wouldn't want a child of mine to suffer for my foolishness."

He could have told her there were modern ways of avoiding such eventualities, but he didn't. Because she was talking sense. And she was absolutely right. He had to stay away from her and stop thinking about her as an attractive woman. She was just a thief who needed an honest job. And he was the man who was going to find it for her.

"All right," he agreed.

"Shake on it," she said, holding out her hand.

Dallas took her hand in his and felt the arc of electricity that charged up his arm. He let her go instantly. He saw the flush in her cheeks and knew he wasn't the only one who had felt it. Like her he refused to acknowledge it.

"Let's go, Angel," he said, heading back into the cave. "I want to make a few phone calls before the day ends."

Angel followed him into the cave, turning on the flashlight to keep away the dark. As she stepped into the icy water, she shivered. She told herself it was only the cold. She forced the fear down her throat and held it at bay. She would survive this calamity on her own, as she had all the others. It was only a matter of taking one moment at a time.

But when Dallas reached back toward her, she took his hand. And held on to it until they reached daylight again.

4

Dallas pulled the truck up to the front door of his house but didn't cut the engine. "You go in and make yourself comfortable," he said to Angel. "I'll be back in a little while. I have to go feed my horse."

"You have a horse? Where?" Angel looked around for a lean-to and spied the roof of a barn-like building in the distance.

"It's over that hill behind the house," Dallas said, confirming Angel's guess. "When I'm not around, one of Adam's cowhands takes care of Red. I prefer to feed and curry him myself when I'm home."

"Can I go with you?"

Dallas shrugged. "I don't know why you'd want to, but sure."

Angel settled back in the seat, and a few minutes later they arrived at the rustic wooden building. The inside of the wooden barn smelled of hay and horse, and Angel took a deep breath as she stepped inside the door. The pungent odors reminded her of the world she had come from.

"This is Red," Dallas said, patting the neck of a sorrel horse that had stuck its head over a stall door the moment they entered the barn. The horse nipped at Dallas's shirt pocket. "Don't have any carrots for you today, boy," Dallas said as he stroked the gelding's jaw.

"He's beautiful," Angel said.

"He and I have been through a lot together."

"Oh?"

"I use him sometimes when I have to track down outlaws where there aren't any roads," Dallas said. "And he's a good cowhorse."

Dallas located a curry comb and brush and began to put a gloss on the animal's already shiny red coat.

Angel stood with her arms looped over the stall door and watched. There was something infinitely comforting about watching Dallas perform a task the same way it had been done over a century ago. Apparently some things never changed.

As she watched, Angel became less aware of what Dallas was doing, and more aware of how he looked doing it. Muscles rippled across his shoulders as he worked. His hands were strong, and the backs of them were dusted with black hair, as were his forearms, revealed by his folded-back shirtsleeves. His chestnut hair darkened and curled at his nape as sweat dampened it. A fine sheen appeared above his lip, and she felt butterflies dance in her belly as he licked it away with his tongue.

In the past Angel had never spent much time contemplating a man. At least not this way. She didn't understand what it was about Dallas that drew her to him. Maybe it was that kiss he'd given her when she'd been wearing no more than her chemise and pantalets. She had only been kissed twice before she met Dallas, and never, never like that. A woman without means in 1864 guarded her virtue because it was the only dowry she had to offer her husband. Angel couldn't afford to let this man from the future sweep her off her feet. Someday she would be going back where she came from, and there a fallen woman wasn't worth a barrel of shucks.

"You've been awfully quiet," Dallas said. "Penny for your thoughts?"

Angel was startled. It was as though he had known she was thinking about him. She said the first thing that came to mind. "We should have spent more time exploring after we saw that flying contraption."

Dallas glanced sharply at her. "For what purpose?"

"Maybe if we'd walked farther in the direction of the other cave opening, we would have found something. I don't know what exactly…"

"A time portal?" Dallas suggested.

"Is that what you call it?" Angel shrugged. She tried to keep the gesture nonchalant, but she felt anything but calm and collected. Her whole life had been turned upside down in the past twenty-four hours. She wanted things back to normal. "I think we should go back again."

There was a long pause during which the only sound was the scrape of the curry comb on Red's flank, followed by the swish of the brush. At last Dallas said, "I don't agree. The sooner you accept the fact you're stuck here, Angel, the sooner you can start learning the things you need to know to survive on your own."

Angel contemplated arguing with Dallas, but decided it would be futile. His mind was made up. She was pretty sure he didn't half believe her story. As far as he was concerned, they had already examined the one route to the past he had suggested might be available. Now he seemed intent on helping her adjust to life in the future.

Angel wasn't ready to give up so easily. She needed to be in San Antonio by the end of the week—or it would be too late. She had promised herself this trip. Not that whether she was there or not would make any real difference. What was going to happen would happen with or without her. But she wanted to be there. It was the least she owed Belinda.

Dallas had given her no choice. She would have to go back to the cave on her own and give things a better, more thorough look. And she was going to have to steal Red to do it.

She hesitated over taking Dallas's horse—stealing horses was a hanging offense in 1864—but she didn't think she had a viable alternative. Dallas's lack of cooperation meant she was going to have to sneak away at night in order to return to the cave. She could never get there on foot before he caught up to her. On the other hand, if she took Red and left him ground-tied outside the cave, it would be more like borrowing than stealing.

"I'd planned to take Red for a short ride before I fed him," Dallas said, interrupting her thoughts. "I guess that'll have to wait now."

"Why?"

"I'd rather not leave you here alone for any length of time," Dallas said.

"Do you think Red would mind carrying double?"

Dallas grinned. "I don't think he'd mind at all."

Angel watched carefully to see where Dallas kept the saddle and bridle stored, and whether Red had any bad habits like biting or kicking that she ought to know about. To her relief the big sorrel horse turned out to be spirited, but good-natured.

Once Dallas was in the saddle, he took his foot out of the stirrup and held out his hand to give Angel a lift up. At first she put her hands on either side of his waist to hold on. As he urged Red to a gallop, it made more sense to slip her arms around Dallas. Unfortunately that brought her breasts flush against his back. She was uncomfortably aware of his warmth, and a strange, tightening sensation that ran from the tips of her breasts down to her belly.

At first she tried to ignore the feelings. When they persisted, she gave up and enjoyed them. She might as well make the most of the few moments they had together. She leaned her cheek against Dallas's back and tightened her grasp across his washboard belly.

Dallas was equally conscious of their close proximity and was cursing himself for having agreed to this folly. He loved having Angel's arms around him, in fact, had been counting on it. The problem was he wanted more.

In the past whenever Dallas had wanted a

woman, he had chosen one who knew the score. They would enjoy some mutually agreeable physical satisfaction and then part ways. He specifically chose women he could walk away from, women who were as unwilling to commit themselves as he was. He stayed away from women whose hearts were vulnerable, women who were not on an equal footing with him.

By his own standards Angel did not qualify as the sort of woman with whom he could have an affair. She was confused. She was vulnerable. And she was apparently inexperienced. Those were three strikes against her. Only he was having a little trouble putting her out of the game.

"Where does that road go?" Angel asked, pointing toward a blacktopped surface.

"There's a little town about three miles south. It's got a bar, a food store and a gas station—just enough amenities to service the fishermen and weekenders who come tubing on the Frio River."

"What's tubing?"

"Folks take the rubber tube from inside a tractor tire and fill it up with air, then use it to sit in while they float down the river," Dallas explained.

"Why would they want to do that?"

"Because it's fun," Dallas said. "In the summer the water's cool and as crystal clear as—as it must have been in 1864. We'll go sometime and you'll see.''

Angel didn't answer him, because she planned to be long gone before she ever had a chance to experience something so frivolous. Didn't people in this century have to *work?*

''Would you like to stop in for a Coke?''

''What's a—''

''A drink of something cold,'' Dallas interrupted. ''As if you didn't know,'' he added.

Angel could tell he was upset with her. It wasn't her fault she didn't know what he was talking about.

''Look, Angel,'' Dallas said. ''Don't you think you've carried this farce about far enough? What are you hoping to gain by pretending to be from the past? It just doesn't make any sense!''

Dallas felt Angel stiffen behind him, then withdraw until only the tips of her fingers clung to his ribs. ''Aw, hell! Why am I bothering? I ought to take you into San Antonio right now and—''

''No! Please don't.'' Angel didn't like the thought of asking for anything, but she couldn't take the chance that Dallas would spirit her any farther from the cave than she already was. ''I don't expect you to believe me,'' she said in a quiet voice. ''It's a little hard for me to accept myself. If you could just be patient with me, I'll do my best not to be a burden to you.'' *In fact, I'll be gone before midnight tonight.*

Dallas snorted in disbelief, but he didn't turn the horse around.

''I'd like that cold drink,'' Angel said. ''If the offer's still open.''

Dallas didn't say anything, just headed Red down the berm of the asphalt road.

Angel sighed in relief when the wood and stone buildings came into sight. This place didn't look too much different from a dozen other one-horse towns she'd been through. However, there were differences that became apparent as soon as they rode up to the structures.

She stepped down off Red, and Dallas threw his leg over Red's neck and slid down to stand beside her.

''Cola machine's over here,'' he said, heading for a tall, boxy-looking object with colored lights on it. He fed in a few coins and a can dropped into a hole at the bottom of the machine. Dallas pulled it out, popped something on the lid and handed it to Angel. Then he got one for himself.

Angel watched him for a moment, then copied him and took a long drink from the hole in the top of the can. She nearly choked on the sweet, fizzy liquid that burned her throat going down. ''What *is* this?'' she demanded, sputtering.

Dallas pounded her on the back until she could catch her breath. "Popular drink of the day," he said by way of explanation.

"It tastes *awful!*"

Dallas laughed. "Maybe to you. But it's plenty well liked nowadays."

"Where can I get a drink of water?"

Dallas stepped over to the drinking fountain beside the cola machine.

Angel stared agog as water spurted from the top of the fountain. "How did you do that?"

He took his boot off the pedal and showed her how the fountain worked.

"That's a pure miracle!"

"Nope. Just modern technology at work."

Angel took a drink and was astonished that the water was cold. "Where do they keep the ice?" She examined the fountain, looking for an opening where blocks of ice could be inserted.

"No ice is used. There are cooling units in the fountain, run by electricity," Dallas said.

Angel shook her head in disbelief. It was a good thing she was going back to her own world. Things here were absolutely mystifying.

"Come on into the store." Dallas put a hand on the small of her back and urged her up the steps into the wooden building. "Maybe we can get you some odds and ends you need."

Angel didn't ask him what he was talking about, just preceded him inside. The store had a somewhat familiar look about it. Wooden shelves lined the walls, and items for sale had been placed in and on glass-enclosed counters for display. While she recognized some objects, others had her completely stymied.

Dallas decided on the spur of the moment to get Angel a couple of extra-large T-shirts to sleep in and some toiletries—toothbrush, toothpaste, comb and brush, shampoo, deodorant—just the basics, that could be carried on horseback. He hadn't counted on Angel's curiosity. Before he could get her out of the store he also had bought a penknife, a bag of potato chips, a package of Twinkies, a Mickey Mouse flashlight, a baseball cap and two pieces of bubble gum, which she insisted they chew right away.

Angel hadn't bought anything she didn't think she would need on her journey—no sense Dallas getting stuck with things he couldn't use. She hugged the bag to her, knowing at least she would have light in the cave, food and some slight protection—the penknife wasn't much—if she should manage to get back to the past.

They spent the entire trip back to Dallas's ranch discussing the appearance of a teenage boy who had walked into the store barefoot and wearing nothing more than a pair of cutoff jeans.

"That's the way a lot of kids dress," Dallas explained.

"Girls too?"

"A girl would be wearing a top of some kind," Dallas conceded.

"Would her limbs be bare from the knee down, the way his were?" Angel demanded incredulously.

"Her legs—and probably her shoulders, back and midriff, too," Dallas said.

"Why that's scandalous!"

"Not these days," Dallas said with a chuckle. "Women are liberated."

Angel gasped. "You mean they were all in prison at one time?"

Dallas laughed. "'Being liberated' is just an expression. I suppose the prevailing social customs seemed as restrictive as being in prison—so women busted out. For the past twenty years or so they've been evening things up between the sexes."

"How?"

"Women can take the same kinds of jobs as men—and get paid the same."

"That sounds fair. Can they own property? And vote?"

"Of course they can!"

Angel smiled. "I could get to like some of these new-fangled ideas."

When they got back to the stable, Angel offered to brush down Red. Dallas agreed so he could go ahead to the house and fix something for supper.

"I'll walk back to the house when I'm done," Angel said. "Don't worry about me."

Once Dallas was gone, Angel made a point of locating the switch in the barn he had used to control the lights and making sure everything was set out so she could quickly saddle up Red when she returned in the middle of the night. She also spent some time petting Red and talking to him so she would be familiar to him when she returned without Dallas. Once everything was as ready as Angel could make it, she returned to the house.

"I'm back," she called as she pulled open the screen door.

"In the kitchen," he answered.

When she found him, Dallas was checking some potatoes with a fork. "They're almost done. Only a few more minutes."

Angel watched Dallas put the potatoes inside a box and punch some buttons. There was an odd chirping sound as bright blue-green numbers came up on a black surface. Then the box began to hum. "What is that?" she asked.

"It's a microwave oven."

Angel tentatively touched the sides of the box. "It isn't hot," she said. "How can it cook anything?"

Dallas grinned wryly. "Well, there are these microwaves in the air inside the box and they get the molecules in the potato to moving real fast and—"

"Stop!" Angel cried, covering her ears. "I don't want to hear any more."

"Come on, then. You can help me set the table."

Angel was never sure what surprise Dallas was going to spring on her next. It was a relief to see that people still used knives, forks, spoons and plates. But sour cream in a *plastic container?* Butter wrapped in *foil sticks?* Bacon bits in a *glass bottle?* Bread crumbs in a *cardboard box?*

Angel couldn't have been more surprised when Dallas pulled lettuce and tomatoes and cucumbers from his refrigerator. "I thought you said it's spring," she accused.

"It is."

"Where did you get all these fresh vegetables that only grow in the summer?" she asked suspiciously.

"These were probably shipped in from Florida or California, or maybe even some other country south of here."

Angel just shook her head and gritted her teeth. There was no sense letting the strangeness of it all get to her. She wasn't going to be here much longer—if everything went as planned. She refused to contemplate what she had to face if she couldn't find her way back to the past.

Dallas saw the tension in Angel's shoulders, the way her jaw worked as if she had her teeth clenched, the unhappy shadows in her blue eyes. Something had happened to rob her of her memory of all this. The least he could do was be patient with her. He was certain that at some point it would all come back to her.

They sat down to a dinner of grilled steak, baked potatoes and a green salad. Angel laughed when Dallas turned out the electric lights in favor of a couple of candles on the table. "Why on earth would you turn out the lights and purposely make it so dark?"

"It's…" He didn't want to say *more romantic*. He had no business romancing her. He settled for saying "So you'll feel more at home."

"Then you ought to have a beer at your elbow," Angel said with a grin.

"I don't drink."

"Not at all?"

"Whiskey sometimes. Liquor dulls the senses," Dallas said. "I like to know what I'm doing all the time."

Angel met his searing gaze, and her heart started thumping. Her grin faded. She stared at his hands, remembering the strength of them smoothing over Red's hide, the gentleness of them cupping her breast.

Dallas recognized Angel's heavy-lidded look. He was no novice at seduction, even if she was. He had to be the one who used good sense here. So he said, "I figure you can take advantage of some courses at the junior college in Uvalde to help you catch up on things. Maybe some art and history and literature. What do you think?"

His abrupt change of subject jolted Angel from the trance into which she had fallen. "College? I only got as far as the eighth grade."

"No problem," Dallas said. "These are courses intended for people who aren't particularly interested in getting a degree, but who want to broaden their knowledge of a subject. We need to be thinking about what career you might pursue."

"I can draw a little," Angel admitted.

Dallas frowned. "I don't know how useful that'll be." Texas had its share of local artists,

and he'd seen a lot of good work at the art fes-
tivals that were held in San Antonio. But "drawing a little" didn't sound like much on which to
build a future. To tell the honest truth, he was
having trouble picturing Angel in any kind of job.

When the meal was finished, Angel helped him
stack the dishes in the dishwasher. She must have
brushed against him a dozen times in the process.
Every time she did his body tautened. The hell of
it was, she seemed to have absolutely no idea
what effect she was having on him. If he didn't
put some space between them, and soon, he
wasn't going to be responsible for the consequences.

"We'd better get some shut-eye. We have a big
day tomorrow."

Angel thought getting to bed early was definitely a good idea, especially since she couldn't
leave until Dallas was asleep. She meekly disappeared into the bedroom with the T-shirts he had
bought for her. In order to put Dallas off guard,
she had to convince him that she was reconciled
to staying with him. She stripped down until all
she had on was a soft cotton T-shirt, and slipped
under the covers. Then she called to him.

"Dallas?"

He answered her from outside the bedroom
door. "What is it, Angel?"

"Uh...could you come in here a minute?"

Dallas hesitated, but not for long. He paused a step inside the door. He had expected her to look alluring, but he wasn't ready for the shock of seeing her looking like that in *his bed*. He reminded himself she was innocent and walked over to stand stiffly beside her. "What can I do for you?"

"I wanted to thank you for everything you've done for me," Angel said.

"Think nothing of it."

"No, I'm really grateful. I didn't want to let that go unsaid." *In case I never see you again.*

"It's been my pleasure," Dallas said.

At that moment he truly meant it. The T-shirt was so big it had slipped down off one shoulder. He could see the dark shadows of her nipples through the thin cotton. He scowled as his body reacted to the sight. He hadn't been this hard and ready with so little provocation since he was a teenage kid, wet behind the ears. It irked him to think he had so little control around her.

Seeing the ferocious look on his face, Angel asked, "What's wrong?"

"Nothing," he muttered. To save his sanity he pulled the blankets up to her neck and said, "Sleep tight," then turned and left the room.

Angel smiled and snuggled down under the covers. Dallas Masterson was a nice man. It was too bad she wasn't going to be around to get to know him better.

Dallas wasn't worried when the light didn't go off in Angel's room. He figured she was sleeping with it on again. He hadn't any intention of going in to check on her. Because he just plain didn't trust himself. It wouldn't take a tiny crook of her little finger and he would be in bed with her. The problem was if that happened he would end up being responsible for her. She had a whole different set of moral values than he was used to dealing with. Bed her and the next step was marriage. Dallas Masterson wasn't a marrying man.

He turned out the lights all over the house, checked the doors to make sure they were locked, then went into the guest bedroom and shut himself inside. He wasn't coming out again until morning—no matter what the temptation. Dallas listened with a sharp ear as, creaking and groaning, the house settled for the night.

Angel didn't even have to guess at the time. The electric clock beside the bed told her it was 11:48. She had promised herself she would be out of Dallas's hair before midnight. That didn't leave her much time.

She had long since packed everything she would need and a few odds and ends for good measure. She'd had to make do with what she had in the bedroom, because she was certain that rooting around in the dark house was liable to wake Dallas. That she couldn't afford to do.

As she silently closed the front door of the house behind her, Angel realized she was going to miss Dallas. She hadn't much trusted anyone in her life—for good reason—but Dallas was different. Maybe it had something to do with reaching out to him in the darkness of the cave, but she felt a closeness to him that she had never felt with any other human being.

Angel shivered when she thought about how angry Dallas was going to be when he discovered that not only had she run away, but she had stolen his horse. She consoled herself with the thought that she wouldn't be around to deal with his wrath.

"Goodbye, Dallas," she whispered as she tiptoed across the porch and down the front steps. "Think of me sometime."

Then she was off and running for the world she had left behind.

5

Angel greeted the approaching cave entrance with a weary smile of relief. It was a starry night, so she hadn't been forced to deal with total blackness, but there was something eerie about being in a time and place where one didn't belong. Red started nervously dancing sideways, and she patted his neck to calm him down.

"There's nothing out there, boy. Nothing but hill country and you and me. Nothing to get spooked about. Take it easy now." It was questionable which of the two of them she was trying more to convince. Red's ears flicked forward and back, as though he was listening to her but distracted by something else.

Was there something out there? Most likely a coyote, she thought. Or maybe a snake slithering away from Red's hooves. "Don't worry, boy," she soothed the anxious horse. "They're as afraid of us as we are of them."

As she stepped down off the gelding at the cave entrance she felt the hairs rise on the back of her neck. She patted the horse again but didn't speak aloud. There was someone here. She felt sure of it. She let the reins trail on the ground, effectively ground-tying the animal, knowing any good cow-horse was trained to stay where he was left.

She had the child's Mickey Mouse flashlight Dallas had bought for her, which made a less-bright light than the flashlight he had used. But it was light. She didn't have to stand there in the dark. Still, she felt reluctant to turn it on. What if there was somebody—some human—around here? She hadn't forgotten the incident that had brought Dallas to her rescue. Angel fingered the penknife she was carrying in her pocket through the rough denim of Dallas's jeans. She stood quietly, listening, but heard nothing. Things just didn't feel right.

Angel started talking to herself. "I have plenty of light. I have a knife. What else do I need? Quit spittin' on the handle, Angel, and get to work!"

She flicked on the flashlight and felt a lot better. The trail of light was easy to follow, sweeping away the dark as she went. Unfortunately the dark closed in behind her. The deeper she went into the cave, the greater her sense of foreboding.

"Stop acting like a hen on a wet griddle," she chastised herself. "There is absolutely *nothing* to be afraid of."

But she *was* afraid. She tried to talk herself out of it. "Give yourself something else to think about, Angel, so you don't spend so much time pondering on the dark. Now there you go again, making note of how black this pit of hell is. Think about something happy. Something wonderful. Like Dallas.

"Now there's a man God spent some time on. Whooee! He is one fine-looking fellow. Never thought you'd fall for a handsome face, Angel, but you sure did go for that Ranger! He—"

Angel distinctly heard a voice. A male voice. And it was behind her. Dallas must have woken up and followed her!

She wasn't about to get caught before she had a chance to look for some sort of portal to the past. She moved faster, almost running. However, she couldn't hold the light steady at that pace, so she missed seeing a dip in the cave floor and lost her balance. She reached out a hand to catch herself as she tumbled. By rolling into the fall, she saved herself hurt, but the flashlight flew out of her hand. The dark was deep and instantaneous as the face of the flashlight hit an outcropping on the rock wall and broke.

"No!" Angel cried. But it was too late. She curled herself into a protective ball, shutting her eyes, as though to shut out the immensity of the dark that surrounded her.

She was six again, and Miss Higgens of the Orphans' Home in Galveston was terribly angry and yelling at her.

"Whatever possessed you to do such a thing, Angela! We have little enough to go around. We can't afford a thief in our midst!"

"But I didn't take anything!" Angel protested.

"I found the biscuits under your pillow," Miss Higgens said. "Are you saying someone else put them there?"

"They must have!" Angel retorted. "My ma taught me better than that. I would never steal—"

"No more than your mother did, I expect," Miss Higgens said disdainfully. "And you see where it got her! In jail, young lady, where she belongs!"

Angel was helpless to deny what Miss Higgens had said. Her mother had stolen—but only food, and only enough to keep them alive.

Then Belinda stepped forward and said, "I did it, Miss Higgens. You're punishing the wrong sister."

"Your loyalty is to be commended, Belinda. But I know who is the real culprit here." She spitted Angel to the spot with a piercing glare.

"I didn't do it," Angel said, her chin tilting mulishly.

"Enough! It won't help to add lying to your list of sins. It's the cellar for you."

Angel started to run, but Miss Higgens grabbed her by the arm in a grip that would have done a vulture proud. She was hauled out back to the root cellar and thrust down inside. The wooden door was dropped closed and a piece of wood pushed through the door handles to seal her inside.

"Let me out!" she cried, pounding against the wood, unmindful of the splinters gathered by her flailing fists. "Please." Her terror was so great that she was even willing to confess and show remorse for a crime she hadn't committed. "Please," she begged. "I'm sorry. I'll never do it again!"

Miss Higgens was ruthless in her determination to stomp out sin. It simply wasn't to be tolerated. She had proof of Angel's transgression. After all, the biscuits had been right there under her pillow. "You will stay in there until you've had a proper chance to reflect upon your sins and find *true* remorse."

Angel didn't know how long she was left in the cellar, but the horrors of the place magnified over time. The cobwebs held poisonous spiders. The bugs crawling over her grew to immense proportions. The mice became rats and threatened to chew off her fingers and toes. And the dark, the oppressive, relentless dark, seeped into her soul.

"Angel? It's me, Belinda. Can you hear me?"

Angel had been wishing so desperately for the sound of another human voice, she thought she was dreaming. She answered, anyway. "Belinda? Is that you?" She leaned her ear against the crack between the cellar doors, so she could hear.

"I'm sorry to be so long in coming," Belinda said. "This is the soonest I could sneak away to visit you. I'm so sorry, Angel. I knew I shouldn't have taken the biscuits. But I was so hungry. It seems like I'm always so hungry!"

"Oh, Belinda. How could you? Mama would—"

"Mama's not here," Belinda said in a sharp voice. "We're on our own, Angel. If we don't take care of ourselves, no one else will. You saw how willing Miss Higgens was to think the worst of you. Our mama was a thief. Nobody, especially not Miss Higgens, is ever going to let us forget it. I'm sorry you got blamed, but I'm not sorry I took the biscuits!"

Belinda left without giving Angel a chance to argue with her. Belinda's words stayed with Angel in the dark and created an epiphany. What good was it to be honest and starve? Why shouldn't she take what she needed? The trick was not to get caught. And she wouldn't, not ever again. Because she would be the one doing the stealing, and she would hide her tracks better than Belinda had.

Miss Higgens had left her in the cellar for twenty-four hours without food or water or—except for Belinda's visit—any other human contact. Angel had come out of the cellar a changed person—harder, more self-reli-ant...and terrified of the dark.

Over the years Angel had lived along a fine line that sometimes crept over into lawlessness. She had taken, when not taking meant going hungry; she had done an honest day's work when it could be had. Despite her epiphany, Angel had never been able to leave behind the notion, ingrained from birth by her mother, that breaking the law was wrong.

Belinda hadn't been so fortunate. The deprivation in their youth had made Belinda crave things, and her scruples had been discarded as she satisfied those cravings. Eventually Belinda had taken to selling herself to live better during the war. Angel had cried the last time she'd seen her sister alive.

Suddenly the cave's darkness was broken by a ray of white light. Dallas had found her. Angel couldn't help the feeling of relief that swept over her. The blackness was gone and with it the memories of a painful past. Here was a man who made her wish she had lived a better life. A man to whom truth and honesty meant something. A good man...whose horse she had stolen, whose trust she had betrayed.

Why did she feel so guilty? She had survived in the past by "feeling true remorse," and then putting the guilt aside. Since childhood, duplicity had held a limited, but necessary, role in her life. Why was she feeling regrets now?

Because she liked and respected Dallas Masterson, and she wanted—needed—his respect. Still, she couldn't set aside the practical side of her nature. The damage was done. She had stolen his horse and left. It made more sense to go forward from here than to turn back.

Angel uncurled slowly and raised a hand to shade her eyes, but she couldn't see the man who stood in the darkness beyond the light. "You might as well come with me," she said, lifting her chin pugnaciously. "I'm not leaving until I explore that exit on the other side of the cave."

"Why, I just might do that, pretty lady," a guttural male voice said. "But I think maybe some of my friends might wanta come along. Hank, Tyrel, Clete," he called. "Come see what I found!"

* * *

Dallas wasn't sure what woke him, but he was suddenly alert, all his senses tuned to danger. He reached down to the floor beside the bed and touched his revolver in the dark. He always kept it nearby, ready at a moment's notice. He listened, but the house was quiet. He left the gun where it was and rose. The feeling of danger had passed; now he felt anxious. He quickly yanked on a pair of jeans before he headed for Angel's bedroom.

The door was ajar. It had been shut last night. He slowly eased it farther open, not certain what to expect, but ready for anything. His gut tightened when he found the bed empty.

"Angel?" The bathroom door was open. That room was empty as well.

He knew she was gone, but that didn't stop him from searching the house. He shoved a frustrated hand through his hair as he tried to imagine where she would have gone, and why. He peered out the front window. The truck was still there—not that he had expected her to try to drive it. But she had done a lot of things he hadn't expected.

She went back to the cave.

He didn't want to think that, but it was the only conclusion that made sense. As he pulled on his socks and boots and threw on a shirt and jacket, he swore at himself for not paying more attention to what she'd said yesterday.

She took my horse!

That thought came out of nowhere, but as soon as it came, he knew it must be true. All the same, he drove his pickup around to the stable to check. Sure enough, Red was gone.

"Damn! Angel Taylor you have a lot to answer for!" he muttered to himself.

She's scared of the dark.

As he drove like a madman toward the cave, he worried about how she was handling the dark. Was she afraid? Would she have the courage to go into that darkened cavern by herself?

She has a flashlight and a knife.

Of course! He had bought them for her at the store. He had thought she was delighted by the penknife and Mickey Mouse flashlight merely because they were unusual. She must have been planning to run away all along! He smiled ruefully. He wondered whether she had tried the Twinkies or the potato chips yet, and how she had liked the taste of them.

She may get lost.

There were three turns to make before she arrived at the water-bound tunnel. He wasn't sure she had been paying close enough attention when they were in the cave together to realize that. What if she accidentally took a wrong turn and got lost? What if her flashlight battery wore down before he found her?

She might find a portal and disappear into the past!

Dallas didn't want to contemplate that possibility, but asked himself why he refused to accept the fact she might really be what she said she was. What if she really had come from the past? What if she did manage to get back?

He would well rid of her. Why, she had been nothing but a bother and a nuisance since he had rescued her from those cowboys. He was a solitary man, used to his privacy. Angel had invaded it and brought…excitement and laughter and a curiosity that made him look at everything with new eyes. She also possessed an innocence that was as seductive as it was charming.

Dallas reminded himself that he had no use for the marrying kind of woman. Hadn't his mother cured him of the notion that true love could last a lifetime? He had watched his father become a shell of his former self after his mother ran away. He had heard his father cry when he read the note his mother had left and had hidden his own sobs of despair and betrayal in his pillow. He would never let a woman do to him what his mother had done to him and his father. No woman was going to wrap herself around his heart and leave him hurting when she decided to see what was over the next horizon. Better just to take what he needed from a woman and avoid the emotional strings that tied a man in knots.

She's gotten under my skin.

So maybe he was a little worried about her. That didn't mean his heart was involved. He worried about abused kids and the homeless, too. That didn't mean he was going to miss her when she was gone. Why, all they'd ever done was talk. He'd hardly even touched the woman.

She would be dynamite in bed!

All right. He admitted he'd had a few daydreams about her. Was it so bad to imagine what it would be like to make love to her? She was a beautiful woman. Her innocence appealed to him. What would it be like to be the first to touch her, to see and feel her responses to the kinds of pleasure a man and woman could share?

She's trouble.

If he was being honest with himself, the truth was he felt something different with Angel than he had felt with any other woman. Maybe it was the protective instincts she aroused in him. Or the way she constantly challenged him and refused to knuckle under to his opinion. There was no doubt about it—she was different. What bothered him most was that he had actually thought once or twice about what it would be like to have her around all the time. Angel had made him yearn for something he had professed not to need—a closer relationship with a woman.

Somehow, in the darkness of that cave, he had formed a bond with Angel that he was finding difficult to untie. He had kept other women at bay with word and deed; Angel had simply slipped past all those fortified walls like fog slips through the mountains.

Dallas hit the brakes, and the truck skidded to a stop as he observed the scenario at the opening of the cave.

''What the hell?''

He reached instinctively for his Colt revolver and swore heatedly when he realized that in his frantic concern for Angel, he hadn't picked it up from beside the bed. *Never, never* had he forgotten his gun! *That's what comes of letting yourself get involved with a woman,* he thought bitterly. The gun would have helped. But it didn't really matter. He wouldn't mind busting a few heads together.

Angel took one look at the leering face of the man as he waved his flashlight back toward his friends, and she reached for the knife in her pocket. In the time it took him to refocus the flashlight on her, she was standing before him with her weight balanced on the balls of her feet, the knife held loosely in her hand. A stench, a sickly sweet smell emanating from the man, curled her nostrils. He was wearing some sort of sleeveless denim jacket that hung open. There was a great deal of flesh visible from the waist up, all of it hairy.

"Now, now," he said. "We don't want anyone to get hurt, do we?"

"No," Angel agreed. "So I suggest you start backing up."

The man just laughed. "I'm not going to hurt you," he said. "Me and my buddies just want to have a little fun."

"Like shoats in a pigpen," she muttered.

"What was that?" he demanded. "You say somethin' about pigs?"

"I'm telling you to back up," she said. "Or face the consequences."

He chuckled. "Little thing like you ought to know better than to try talking back to a big fella like me."

Angel moved without warning, slicing at the big man's naked arm. The cut was shallow, but the stranger yowled as if she'd gutted him, and he dropped the flashlight to clutch his wound.

Angel grabbed the light and ran while he was still grappling with his bloody arm.

"She's comin' your way!" the man shouted to his friends. "Stop her! That bitch cut me with a knife!"

Knowing she was armed kept the other three men at a distance. Angel never slowed down, just waved the knife at them, feinted as though she were going to attack, and then ran like the devil. By the time she reached the cave opening, the man she had wounded had reached his friends, and she could hear him exhorting them to go after her, ranting at them for their cowardice in the face of "one tiny little woman."

Once out of the cave, Angel used the flashlight to search for Red. He had drifted off a ways, munching grass—near four strange, menacing machines that she had not noticed in the shadows when she'd arrived. She edged warily around them to reach Red, then threw herself into the saddle and lit a shuck out of there, back toward Dallas and safety.

Mere seconds later she looked over her shoulder to see that the men had mounted the machines as though they were horses. The roaring sound behind her was more terrifying than the scream of a cougar. She looked back and saw that the heads of the four men had been completely encased in large, dark objects, becoming featureless. Indeed the men and machines seemed like exotic one-eyed beasts chasing after her.

It became very clear, very fast, that she could not outrun them. When Angel saw a set of headlights, she veered toward them. Hopefully this was someone who would help her; she was no worse off if it wasn't. She was counting on providence to arrange for her rescue. Otherwise she would fend for herself. These four men might overwhelm her, but they would pay dearly before they did.

Dallas took one look at Angel riding hell-bent for leather on Red, chased by four rough-looking men on motorcycles, and reached for his gun. When he found it missing, he realized he was going to have to rely on cunning and intelligence—and luck—if he hoped to get Angel out of this without anybody getting hurt. Of course if he ended up having to use a little muscle along with his brain, he wasn't going to mind one bit.

He stepped down from the cab and went to stand just beyond the front lights of the pickup, which he had left on after he killed the engine.

Angel yanked Red to a sliding halt, threw herself out of the saddle and headed toward the truck on the run. "Help!" she cried. "I need help."

"Over here, Angel," Dallas said in a quiet voice.

She flew into his arms and he gave her a quick, hard hug before putting her away from him. "Go stand over by the truck, but stay out of the light."

The appearance of the truck had changed things for the men on motorcycles. They skidded their bikes to a stop on the fringes of the light and revved the engines threateningly.

"This is none of your business," the wounded man shouted from the darkness. "Get back in your truck, mister, and get outta here."

"I'm making it my business," Dallas said. "You can make something out of it if you want to, but I won't go down easy. Any of you boys wants to try me, come ahead."

Finally one of the motorcycle engines went dead, and the man Angel had wounded with her knife stepped into the light.

"I've got me a grudge to settle with that bitch, even if I have to go through you to do it."

For the first time, in the light from the truck headlights, Angel saw the face of the huge man who had confronted her in the cave. He had a mustache that hung down and hid his lips. His nose was too big for his face and his eyes too small. His hair hung limp and greasy.

Her gaze drifted down over the rest of him.

Obscenities were written on his denim jacket, and
his hairy belly hung down over jeans that had
some kind of metal studs along the outside seam.
There were tattoos on his arms, like the black
markings she had sometimes seen on the slaves—
now freed by President Lincoln—who had come
from Africa. He looked mean and in no mood to
be reasonable.

"You and me," the wounded man said. "Winner gets the girl."

Dallas felt the killing rage rise up inside him
and controlled it. This man had threatened Angel,
frightened her, wanted to rape her. The hair stood
up on his nape; he was a feral animal challenged
for his mate. "Fine," he said, his voice cold and
hard. "You and me. Winner gets the girl."

Dallas stepped into the light.

Angel saw the sudden wariness in the biker's
face. He clearly hadn't been expecting to face
someone of Dallas's stature. He still had the advantage of reach and weight. He stepped forward,
hands fisted and held up to protect his face. Dallas
lifted his hands into daunting fists, as well. Angel
watched the two men circling each other, looking
for weaknesses and an opening to attack.

The biker struck first.

Dallas dodged the blow but felt knuckles graze
his cheek as he hit up under the biker's chin. He

heard the man's teeth click as his head rolled with the punch. He managed a solid hit to the ribs before the biker closed on him. The man was huge, and his bearlike grip was squeezing the breath and the life out of Dallas. Desperate, he kicked the biker in the shin. Dallas slipped out of the man's grasp as the biker limped backward in agony.

Dallas didn't give the man a chance to recover, but moved inside his guard with a quick right to the eye and a left to the solar plexus.

The biker gasped as Dallas's punch forced the air out of his lungs. He swung wildly, and Dallas ducked and came up punching again.

It was over quickly, as the biker dropped to his knees, then sagged to all fours. "Enough," he gasped, blood dripping from cuts on his mouth and cheek.

Dallas grabbed him by the scruff of the neck and yanked him to his feet. "If I ever see you around these parts again, I'll make sure you spend your time here in jail. Is that clear?"

"Yeah," the biker mumbled.

"Now you and your friends get on your bikes and get out of here."

Dallas waited while the bikers revved their engines and then took off, wheels spinning. As the roar faded and the quiet took over, he turned to Angel. He had worked off some of his anger in the fight, but his adrenaline was still pumping. He stalked over and stood spread-legged in front of her. He wanted some answers.

Angel had crossed her arms protectively over her breasts. She looked vulnerable, and suddenly he realized what might have happened to her if he hadn't arrived in time. He grabbed her shoulders and demanded, "Are you okay? Did any of them hurt you?"

"No. I'm fine." She reached up and gently touched the bruise forming on his cheek. "I think you're the one who came off a little the worse for wear."

He was furious because even now, angry as he was, frightened as he'd been for her, he wanted her. "Do you realize what would have happened to you if—"

She smoothed the hair back from his forehead. "Nothing happened."

"Because you were damned lucky!" he said. He wanted her to stop touching him; he wanted her to touch him a helluva lot more. "What were you doing in that cave?"

She straightened the collar on his shirt. "Exactly what you think I was doing."

His hold tightened on her arms. "You have no business in that cave. I want you to stay out of there."

"No."

Exasperated, he shook her. "Stop being stubborn."

She put her hands flat against his chest and looked up into his fierce eyes. "Don't you understand? This is your world. I have to return to mine."

All he knew was that he didn't want her going anywhere without him. "Don't go back," he said. "Stay here with me." He didn't know where the words had come from. He wished he hadn't spoken them, but he had. He waited with bated breath for her answer.

"I have to go back."

"Why? What's back there that's so important to you?"

She reached into her jeans pocket, pulled out a piece of folded paper and extended it to him.

Dallas had to let go of her to take the paper. He wasn't sure what he had expected, but it wasn't a WANTED poster. "Who is Jake Dillon to you?"

"My brother-in-law. He married my sister, then talked her into helping him rob a bank in San Antonio. She was killed and so was a bank teller. The posse caught up to Jake in Del Rio. He's being hung on Saturday. He's the reason my sister is dead. I want to be there to see him hang."

"Bloodthirsty little thing, aren't you?"

"How would you feel about a man who was directly responsible for the death of someone you loved?"

He already had his answer. He had wanted to kill. Could he condemn her for wanting to see vengeance done by the law?

Dallas suddenly realized that what he was holding wasn't a copy, that it appeared genuine. Yet it wasn't old and yellowed. The date on the poster was 1864. Here was the proof he had lacked. He could have the poster checked to make sure, but he didn't want to have to make any explanations to any authorities. If she really was from the past, perhaps she deserved one last chance to get back.

He sighed. "All right. We'll go back through the cave one more time. But I want your promise that if we don't find what we're looking for, that's it. No more sneaking off in the middle of the night. You'll stay with me until you learn what you need to know to survive in this century. Agreed?"

She looked up into his eyes and said, "All right. It's a deal."

She stood on her tiptoes and kissed him on the mouth.

Dallas put his fingers to his lips, surprised at

how much they tingled from such a slight touch.
"What was that for?"

"That was to thank you for coming to the rescue."

He leaned down and kissed her back, just a slight touch of lip to lip, leaving them both yearning for more.

"What was that for?" she asked breathlessly.

"I was sealing our bargain with a kiss," he murmured against her lips. "There's no backing out now."

"No backing out," she agreed.

6

Dallas emerged from the darkness of the cave into the sunlight with somewhat less care this time. He had been here once before and found nothing. He was nearly certain they would not find a portal to the past. But he had promised Angel he would bring her here. So he had.

He reached out a hand to her. "Let me help you."

Angel allowed Dallas to pull her the last few feet up out of the stream within the cave and onto dry land. "It looks the same as it did before," she said as she studied the surrounding terrain.

Dallas narrowed his eyes against the glare of the noonday sun. He had that same eerie feeling that things weren't quite right. The grass was yellow, not green, and crackled under his boots. It seemed more like late fall than spring. But then, he had been through all this before. He looked up at a cloudless sky, expecting any moment to see a jet contrail. However, the sky was a clear blue as far as the eye could see.

"Which way should we go?" Angel asked.

Dallas shrugged. "Your guess is as good as mine." He pointed west. "That's the direction of the cave opening that got dynamited. I suppose we might as well head that way."

Angel nodded her agreement and Dallas took off, not waiting to see if she followed him. He couldn't describe his feelings, exactly. He felt foolish, of course, because he simply couldn't believe they were going to find themselves in the past. He also felt frustrated that Angel seemed so desperate to return to her life before she had met him. And he felt anxious. His intuition had kept him alive in more than one dark alley. And his intuition told him they were heading into trouble.

"Dallas?"

He paused and turned to Angel. She was pointing at something in the brush to the left. Her eyes were wide and she had her lower lip clasped in her teeth. He followed the extension of her hand and felt his flesh get up and crawl at what he saw.

"Is that what I think it is?" he asked.

Angel nodded. "It looks like my rucksack all right. Or what's left of it."

Dallas unconsciously touched the Colt .45 at his hip as they moved together toward the leather bag. His eyes scanned the horizon looking for an enemy he could only imagine. A band of raiding

Comanches? Outlaws? Renegade Confederate soldiers? Every muscle in his body was tensed for action. He knew enough history to have a healthy respect for the dangers of the past. If that was where they were.

Angel knelt to examine the scraps of leather. All around were pieces of shredded paper that had been her pencil drawings and rags of cloth that had been her clothes. "It's mine," she said in a quavery voice. "They've destroyed everything."

Dallas put his hands on her shoulders and raised her up. He watched her fight the tears pooling in her eyes. "I'm sorry, Angel. You can always replace what they ruined."

She met his gaze and said, "They destroyed all my drawings of my sister and my fiancé."

Which were not replaceable, he realized. Dallas felt a sudden rage at the men who had done this, who had attacked Angel and destroyed without thought the things that meant so much to her. The ragged sound of Angel's voice tore him from his thoughts.

"Do you think finding my rucksack means we're in the past now?"

Dallas frowned. "I don't know. If we did somehow manage to make our way into the past, why did it happen this time and not the last? We didn't do anything differently that I'm aware of."

Angel gnawed on her lower lip, trying to find an explanation for the inexplicable. "Does it really matter how we got here, so long as we're here?"

"It does if we—I—hope to go back."

"Oh."

Dallas put up a hand to shade his eyes as he looked back the direction they had come. Suddenly, nothing looked familiar. He felt a stunned breathlessness as he realized the darkened cave opening was no longer there, only a blank wall of stone. "It's gone."

"What's gone?" Angel asked.

Dallas nodded toward the spot where the cave entrance had been.

Angel gasped. "How could it just…disappear like that?"

Dallas fought the urge to walk over and put his hand on the stone to physically experience what his eyes told him had happened. He felt a sickening lurch in his stomach. This was too weird for words. If what he suspected was true, he and Angel had passed through some portal of time *and it had closed behind them.*

Dallas's mouth flattened into a thin line. He hadn't believed they would end up in the past, and he certainly hadn't counted on having a problem finding his way back to the future. He took a step back toward the stone wall, then stopped. Closer examination was not going to reveal what plainly wasn't there.

His inclination was to stop right now and figure out how to get back where he had come from. But if the portal was there—and he refused to believe it wasn't—then it would still be there after he had escorted Angel to San Antonio for the hanging. That was a deadline that they knew was finite. After the hanging he could come back and figure it all out.

He met Angel's blue eyes with a somber stare. "It looks like you got your wish, Angel," he said. "Apparently we've crossed over some portal to the past. Now what?"

"There's probably some good explanation for why the cave opening isn't there any more," Angel said in a placating tone. "As soon as we can figure out what we did to get here, we'll know how to get back. Or rather, how to get you back. As long as we are here, why don't we head for San Antonio. We can think just as well while we're walking."

Dallas's mouth twisted wryly. "I suppose that makes sense." He looked over at the solid stone wall one last time. "Standing around here isn't going to accomplish anything."

This time, Angel led the way. "I've been to

San Antonio a couple of times," she said. "It's not a bad walk from here. Maybe sixty miles."

That was an hour's drive in Dallas's truck. And two long days on foot. At least they had supplies, food and water that he'd packed as a precaution before they went into the cave. And he had his gun. Dallas told himself he was just taking a little camping trip. Nothing to it. They would be fine. And when they got to San Antonio...

The enormity of his situation hit Dallas all at once. *He was in the past!* As fantastic as it seemed, Angel had been telling the truth about where she had come from. Dallas felt exhilarated. He was living an adventure that most men could only dream about. He would see San Antonio as it had been near the end of the Civil War. He would witness a public hanging in the town square. That is, if they ever reached San Antonio.

Dallas dismissed the possibility that they wouldn't make it. Angel certainly didn't seem to be entertaining any fears about the forthcoming journey. But he couldn't help asking, "Are you sure you know where you're going?"

She grinned. "For the first time in nearly a week I know exactly where I am."

Dallas was willing to follow where she led. He was impressed that evening as he watched her choose a campsite along the Guadalupe River and start a fire. "You've done this before," he said.

Angel smiled at him. "Dozens and dozens of times. You forget, this is my world."

Dallas felt a stab of regret. Angel seemed perfectly happy here. It certainly didn't look like she had any plans to return with him to the future. Assuming that he could return. He didn't want to think about that right now. Or about what his life would be like in the future without Angel in it.

Dallas had done some camping, but this was different. There was no civilized town over the horizon, no escape from the elements or the dangers of this land. He knew he ought to be afraid, but somehow the fear never came. Instead, he felt solace, a kind of peace he had never experienced in the future. Which was crazy. He didn't try to explain it; he simply enjoyed it.

After supper, Dallas sat back against a sun-warmed stone with a tin cup of coffee in his hand and realized he had never felt so content. "This is really wonderful," he murmured.

Angel sat cross-legged near the fire, her coffee cup warming her hands in the evening chill. The night sky was filled with stars that seemed timeless. "I missed this when I was in the future," she admitted. "The spaces without people, I mean. And the quiet."

A coyote howled in the distance and was joined by a chorus of mournful yelps.

"That doesn't sound so quiet to me," Dallas said.

Angel smiled. "The sounds in my time are natural. Crickets and frogs. The rustling of leaves. Even the coyotes. They're not as harsh to the ear as the ring of a phone, or the whine of a motorcycle."

Dallas opened his mouth to agree with her, but froze when the quiet was pierced by a gunshot. He dropped his coffee cup, leaped up and kicked sand into the fire, then grabbed Angel around the waist and headed for cover. Their peace was gone. The clamor of a dangerous civilization had intruded.

"You expecting company?" Dallas hissed into Angel's ear.

"No."

"Any suggestions who that might be?"

"No."

"Then I suggest we pack up and get out of here."

They matched actions to words and quietly and efficiently returned what they had removed from Dallas's backpack and set off in the dark toward their destination. Dallas hadn't realized how complete the darkness would be. There was no distant halo of light that signaled a town. There was only the light from the stars and a rising moon to show them where to step.

Suddenly Dallas felt a surge of admiration for the woman who followed in his footsteps, the woman whose hand he held tightly in his own. He knew her fear of the dark was genuine. Yet she seemed unperturbed by the vastness of the land over which they walked, the immense noth-ingness that was Texas before man had conquered its untamed reaches.

They walked for several hours in silence, until Dallas was sure they weren't being pursued by whatever danger lay behind them. At last he slowed and finally stopped in the hollow of a hill. "We'll rest here."

"I'm not tired," Angel said.

Dallas grinned wryly. "I am." He dropped the heavy pack he carried and sank to the ground near a lone mesquite tree, pulling her down beside him.

"Are you cold?" he asked.

She shivered in response.

Dallas lifted her into his lap and enfolded her in his arms. She laid her head on his chest and snuggled up closer to him. Dallas smoothed the hair away from her forehead. "Do you think you can sleep?"

She yawned. "Umm-hmm."

He settled himself back against the tree and pulled her close. It felt good to hold her in his arms, and he realized he'd been wanting to do it for a long time. Maybe this would be the last time. Tomorrow when they arrived in San Antonio she would take her leave of him. He would have to find his way back to the future alone. Somehow, that didn't frighten him. What frightened him was the thought of a lifetime without the woman he held in his arms.

He thought about making love to her, awakening her to the physical pleasures he knew a man and a woman could find together. Yet how could he take her virginity and leave her to face the consequences alone? A fallen woman. A pariah in her time. He couldn't—wouldn't—do that to her.

Dallas tightened his arms around Angel and groaned as her soft breasts nestled against him. It was going to be a long night. He closed his eyes, willing himself to sleep, knowing it would be a long time before he found respite from the knowledge of what had happened to him today.

Angel wasn't sure what woke her. Perhaps the trill of a mockingbird flying overhead. Perhaps the ray of sunlight that glimmered over the hill. Perhaps the contrasting warmth of Dallas's breath against her brow in the chill morning air. She only knew she had awakened with a sense of rightness in this man's arms.

The signs of a violent life marked Dallas's face even in sleep. Angel was convinced he would do very well in her time and wondered whether she should try to convince him to stay. She tried to imagine him living without the modern conveniences she had learned so much about. And had to admit it would be harder for him to adjust to living without, than for her to accept the luxuries the future provided.

Angel frowned. Why was she thinking at all about the future any more? She belonged in the past. It was her world. There was no sense contemplating a life somewhere else.

Only it wasn't the conveniences Angel knew she would miss. It was Dallas. She felt a rush of tenderness as she perused the face of the man who held her in his arms. Those ridiculous curly lashes. Chestnut hair shot with golden sunlight. His broken nose. Lips that could be hard, or oh, so soft and giving.

She reached out a fingertip and traced the width of his mouth. Intent on what she was doing, Angel didn't notice as Dallas's lids lifted to reveal watchful hazel eyes. When his lips parted, she leaned forward and pressed her mouth against his. And was astonished at the reaction she got.

Angel let her eyelids sink closed as Dallas's mouth molded itself to hers. His tongue slid along the edge of her lips until she opened to him. She felt a sense of urgency that grew from the knowledge that their time together was coming to an end.

Angel felt the pull of desire so strong it frightened her. She put her hands against Dallas's shoulders to push him away, but they quickly slid up around his neck and tangled in his hair. She wanted this. She needed this.

For long moments, Angel was lost in the kiss. She wasn't aware of the exact moment Dallas turned her beneath him. She yielded easily when his knee nudged her thighs apart and he settled himself between her legs. It was not until she felt the thrust of his hips that she realized how far she had let things go.

She turned her head away from his seeking mouth, and in a raspy voice said, "This is wrong. Dallas, we can't do this."

"Why not?" he demanded.

His eyes were heavy-lidded, darkened by desire. Angel realized she had been unfair to let Dallas believe she was willing to give herself to him when she was not. But in the beauty of the dawn she had wished...

"Because I'll be staying here," she said in a

steady voice. ''And you'll be going back. It's better if we don't—''

He grasped a fistful of her hair and forced her to face him. ''I want you. If this is all the time we'll ever have together, I want it. I want to remember you like this—''

Angel looked up into his eyes and realized she wanted him as much as he wanted her. But it wasn't only herself she had to think about. If she had a child…Dallas's world might accept and forgive. Her world would not.

She begged for understanding with her eyes. At last she realized she would have to say the words. ''I can't.''

Dallas released her and lurched to his feet. He stood with his back to her, legs spread, balled fists on his hips.

Angel saw the tension in his shoulders. She stood shakily and brushed the grass from her clothes, not sure what she could, or should, say.

''Dallas?''

He whirled and she gasped at the rigid set of his jaw, the way his eyes still glittered green and gold with desire. His chest heaved. Every muscle was taut as though he were straining against a tether. She watched him visibly rein the raw passion that had him drawn tight as a bowstring.

His struggle intensified her own yearning. "Dallas?"

"Don't look at me like that," he warned. "Or you're liable to get what you're asking for."

Angel lowered her lids to hide the need she didn't seem to be able to control, the flare of desire that made her feel weak in the knees. When she looked up again his face was a mask behind which his feelings were shuttered.

They had coffee and breakfast and took care of their personal needs without another word spoken. Even so, it was not an unpleasant silence. It was not wrong for Dallas to desire her, or for her to feel desire in return, Angel thought. If only the circumstances were different, what had happened between them would have been a prelude to something deeper, something permanent.

But the circumstances were different. Which made any relationship between them quite impossible.

Dallas lifted the backpack onto his shoulders, looked up to find the sun and asked, "South?"

"Southeast," Angel replied.

It was dusk by the time they reached the outskirts of San Antonio. They had talked on and off over the afternoon about what Dallas could expect to see. Still, he was enthralled to encounter the first *jacales*—wooden-sided huts—and adobe buildings. He marveled at the old Spanish missions that in 1992 provided tourist attractions in San Antonio. And, of course, he felt the same tightness in his chest he felt every time he stepped inside the dim, shadowy interior of the Alamo.

It was strange to realize the layout of the roads was already set in 1864. Later they would simply be paved and these adobe and wood buildings replaced with brick and stone. The muddy San Antonio River that ran through the city would one day become another tourist attraction, the River Walk.

Dallas stared until his eyes glazed. It was all here, everything that would one day be sprawling San Antonio. Only now it was confined to a small area of adobe and wood-frame homes and a central square where cows and horses and even chickens could be seen on the streets.

Quaint.

Dallas felt the silly smile on his face, but didn't fight it. San Antonio looked like a movie set for a B Western, right down to the American cowboys and Spanish vaqueros in buckskin chaps. He could hear the twangy sound of a Spanish guitar coming from the open door of a white-washed adobe cantina.

"What do you think?" Angel asked.

His grin broadened. "I feel like Alice in Won-

derland, like I've stepped into a hole and everything's wacky."

"*Wacky?*"

"Strange. Weird. Unbelievable."

Angel grinned back. "I know the feeling."

They laughed together. The smiles hadn't left
their faces when someone bumped into Dallas
from behind.

"Look where you're going!" a rough voice
growled.

Dallas didn't have time to turn around before
he was shoved out of the way. He might have let
the insult pass, except the drunken cowboy also
shoved Angel. She lost her balance and would
have fallen except Dallas caught her. Even that
might not have been a disaster, only her hat fell
off, and her white gold hair fell to her waist.

"Heeeey," the drunken man slurred. "Tha'sa
woman."

The drunken man was still weaving in front of
them, a leer on his face, when he was joined by
several of his friends.

It took a moment for Dallas to realize they were
the same gang of cowboys who had confronted
Angel at the cave.

Angel realized the danger of the situation at the
same time he did. She had already started backing
away when one of the more sober members of the

group said, "That's him. That's them. That's the low-down dirty dog who stole the girl from us at the cave."

"I thought we'd blown them to smithereens," one said.

"Guess not!" another hooted.

"Shut up!" one of the more sober ones said. "You want to get us in trouble with the law?"

They shushed each other with fingers to lips until they broke out laughing, and their attention once again focused on the man and woman before them.

"She's even purtier than I remember," one said.

Dallas shoved Angel behind him and faced the six men. "You boys better move along."

One of them laughed. "Hell, no. We ain't movin' unless the little señorita comes along."

"She stays with me," Dallas said. His voice would have cut glass.

The cowboys were too drunk to care.

Dallas was already considering how best to disable the closest man when a deep voice behind him said. "That's all, boys. Game's over."

Dallas glanced over his shoulder and saw not the man behind him, but the badge—which consisted of the same cinqo peso coin with a star cut into it that the Texas Rangers still wear in 1992.

The cowboys shoved each other in the ribs and backed off. A few moments later they were gone.

Dallas turned to greet the gray-haired lawman.

"You folks new in town?" the Texas Ranger asked.

"Just got in," Dallas admitted. He noticed the Ranger eyeing his revolver and realized it was a model from the late 1870s. It wouldn't be issued for another ten years at least.

"Unusual firearm you have there," the Ranger said.

Dallas put his hand on the butt of the gun, but he didn't offer to remove it from the holster. "It's a special issue."

"Mind if I take a look at it?" the Ranger asked.

Dallas debated the wisdom of handing over the gun, but had faith in the Ranger to treat him fairly, even if he found the gun suspicious. Besides, he felt a certain affinity for the man since he was also a Texas Ranger. Dallas handed the gun over, butt first.

The Ranger looked it over, admiration clear in his eyes. "This is a nice weapon. Who'd you say made it?"

"I didn't."

The Ranger didn't ask again. Instead he said, "You here for the hanging?" His eyes slid to the gallows that had been constructed on the town square.

Dallas nodded. "Didn't know if I'd make it in time."

"First thing tomorrow morning," the Ranger said.

Dallas and Angel exchanged grave looks. "We'll be there," Dallas said. He saw Angel shiver as she gazed at the hangman's noose that was already set in place.

The Ranger handed Dallas his Colt and he slid it into the holster. "You looking for a place to spend the night?" the Ranger asked.

"Could be."

"Mrs. Mortensen's boarding house is down the street. Good food and clean beds. No lice." The Ranger tipped his hat to Angel and said, "So long, ma'am. You folks be careful now."

The Ranger sauntered away down the boardwalk, past a mercantile store, the blacksmith, the saddler and the bank. He finally settled into a rocking chair on the shaded veranda in front of the adobe jail.

Dallas released a breath of air he hadn't realized he'd been holding. Everything that had just happened seemed like something from a movie script.

"Shall we go find the boarding house?" he asked Angel.

She shrugged. "We might as well."

The boarding house, as it turned out, was right across the street from the jail. It was a two-story wood-frame building with Victorian furniture, feather ticking in the mattresses and a pitcher and washbowl on the table beside the four-poster bed. The necessary was out back. Baths and a barber could be found down the street.

Dallas's mouth gaped when Mrs. Mortensen asked for payment in advance, and he realized he had nothing that vaguely resembled the money used in 1864.

Angel promptly sat down and removed her left boot. She grinned at Dallas as she revealed a secret compartment in the heel that contained a wad of Confederate bills.

"I've been saving it for an emergency," she explained.

Dallas just shook his head and allowed Mrs. Mortensen to show them to their rooms.

"I'll meet you later and we can go downstairs together for supper," Angel said. Then she disappeared into her room.

Dallas wondered if Angel had felt as disoriented in the future as he did in the past. He decided her culture shock must have been worse than his. At least he knew what to expect in the past. She'd had no inkling of what the future held in store. He kept telling himself this was only temporary. There was a portal somewhere that would take him back to the life he had left behind.

But he worried about how he would find it when the time came.

It was after dark when Angel finally knocked on his door. He opened it to find her dressed in a full-length skirt and pin-striped white blouse.

She blushed and stammered, "Mrs. Mortensen loaned these to me. They belonged to her daughter."

Dallas was stunned by how right Angel looked in the old-fashioned clothing. Even though the lace-edged blouse covered her to the neck and wrists, and the flounced skirt concealed her all the way to the ankles, he didn't think he'd ever been more entranced by a woman.

Angel had put her hair up into a kind of bun, but wisps of hair escaped around her ears and at her neck. Dallas had the urge to thread his fingers in it and set it free. He swallowed back the desire he felt. She was off-limits. He could look, but not touch.

And that made him ache ten times worse.

"Let's go," he said. His voice was harsh with the need he felt.

Angel sent a glance upward under lowered lashes, but it was enough to recognize the approval in Dallas's eyes. Approval and something else...desire. She felt regret for what could never be. If only... If wishes were wings, pigs could fly. Angel took the arm Dallas offered and let him escort her downstairs.

They were eating steak and fried potatoes in the common dining room of the boarding house when they heard the explosion.

"Sounds like the bank's being robbed again!" Mrs. Mortensen cried. "That's how they did it last time. Blew up the safe and—"

Dallas was already up and headed for the door. Only, it wasn't the bank. The roof of the jail across the street was on fire. In the light of the flames, Dallas saw what he supposed was the Texas Ranger he had met earlier in the day lying facedown on the ground. Apparently the explosion had knocked him out.

There was a ragged hole in the jail wall beneath the barred window. Dallas saw shadowy figures struggling to get the iron bars off the window of the jail. A rope had been slung around the window and tied to the horn of a saddle. A man on horseback was urging the animal to pull. Suddenly, the window came loose, and several men helped free the prisoner.

"That's Jake Dillon!" Angel cried. "He's escaping."

Dallas acted instinctively to stop the jailbreak. His gun was already out of the holster as he raced across the street. "Texas Ranger!" he shouted. "Stay where you are and put your hands up!"

As he approached, Dallas recognized the men as the same ones who had held Angel at bay. That explained why they'd had dynamite on hand to blow up the cave opening! He should have known, should have suspected.

"Get moving!" one of the men shouted at Jake. "I'll take care of the Ranger." He turned and fired his revolver at Dallas.

Instincts honed by years of danger caused Dallas to drop to the ground even as he fired back at the other man.

The cowboy cried out and clutched his chest.

"He got Slim!" one of the outlaws shouted.

Angel gasped when she saw Dallas go down at the same time the outlaw fired. She ran into the street just as the outlaws were mounting their horses. The few pins in her hair didn't survive the jouncing and the mass of gold streamed down her back, highlighted by the fire.

"It's the girl!" one outlaw shouted.

"Grab her!" another yelled.

It was all over in a matter of seconds. One of

the outlaws leaned down and circled Angel under the arms, hauling her up and throwing her face-down over the front of his horse.

Dallas took careful aim at the escaping prisoner and fired. It was apparent from the hue and cry of the band of outlaws that his bullet had found its mark.

"Jake's bought it!"

"Damn that Ranger's hide!"

They were milling in a circle, unsure whether to come back to seek revenge, or make good their escape with the girl. Dallas took advantage of their indecision, stole the nearest horse from the hitching rail and galloped directly into the tightly knit band of outlaws, causing their horses to shy and rear.

It was dark and he had grabbed Angel from the outlaw's horse and was riding out of town before the outlaws fully realized what had happened. Furious at the Ranger's interference, they kicked their horses into pursuit.

Dallas slowed just long enough to settle Angel behind him on the wiry mustang, then urged his mount back to a run. He put two hard miles between him and the band of outlaws before he slowed the winded gelding to a trot and then a walk.

"Horse needs a breather," he said curtly.

"Dallas, I—"

"What the hell were you doing out in the street!" he demanded.

"Checking to see if you were dead!" she retorted.

"You could have been killed!"

"I wasn't!"

"What the hell am I going to do with you now?" he demanded.

"Let me off here. I can manage fine on my own," she said.

Angel had already slid off the rump of the mustang, and Dallas quickly joined her on the ground. He grabbed her by the shoulders and said, "How can I go back to the future knowing you're not safe here?"

"I'll be fine," she assured him.

"Those men will be after you now."

"It's a big state," she said. "I'll go where they can't find me. Don't worry about me. You're the one in danger. We need to get back to the cave. Now that you've killed Jake, they won't stop hunting until they find you and kill you."

Dallas took off his hat and thrust a hand through his hair. "What a mess," he muttered.

Angel put a tentative hand on his shoulder. "Shouldn't we at least head for the cave?"

Dallas was torn, but what she said made sense.

If worse came to worst, he'd take her back to the future with him whether she wanted to go or not. "All right," he said. "Let's go."

The trip was quicker on horseback. They stopped only to relieve themselves and to drink some water from the river at dawn. It was nearly noon by the time they reached the cave. Or rather, the spot where the cave was supposed to be.

It wasn't there.

Dallas had known for some time that they were being followed. The size of the dust cloud left no doubt in his mind that it was a group of men. It didn't take much imagination to figure out which men. He kicked his leg over the horse's neck, then helped Angel dismount.

His hands lingered at her waist. Her disheveled look made her seem vulnerable. One sleeve of the lacy blouse was torn at the shoulder. Her skirt, which had been hiked up over her knees on horseback revealing old-fashioned high-button shoes, was layered with fine dust.

She looked like a damsel in distress, and he wanted desperately to rescue her. Only he would have to stay in this world to do it.

He was willing to make the sacrifice. There was no one who would miss him if he stayed here, if he simply disappeared. Why not? It made sense. He would—

Dallas felt the awful pain before he heard the shot. His leg crumpled under him, and since he was holding Angel, he pulled her down with him into a ravine that gave them some protection.

"You've been shot!" she cried. She touched his leg and her hand came away stained red with blood. "Oh, God, Dallas!"

He pulled the bandanna from around his neck with hands that weren't as steady as he wished. He was losing blood fast from the bullet wound in his thigh.

"Tie this around my leg, above the wound," he instructed Angel.

Another woman would have fainted, he thought, or been hysterical and unable to help. Angel simply did as she was told. When she finished, she looked up at him and he felt something deep inside him melt and flow. It was too bad they probably weren't going to live too much longer. It would have been interesting to see how they fared together in the years to come.

One of the outlaws made the mistake of showing himself, and Dallas shot him.

"Give yourself up!" another outlaw shouted. "You're gonna die of thirst out there anyway. Why make it harder on yourselves? We ain't gonna kill you, Ranger. We just want the girl."

Dallas didn't bother to answer. There was no

question of giving Angel up. But the outlaws had a point. He and Angel didn't have water or food. And there was no escape across the plains without getting shot.

The next half hour passed slowly as the sun rose to its zenith. Dallas and Angel lay close together in a narrow ravine that provided cover from the outlaws. Dallas had grasped Angel's hand, and he held onto it as the lifeblood seeped out of him. He intended to fight, but wounded as he was, the chances were slim that they would escape the outlaws.

"Dallas."

The combination of urgency and wonder in Angel's voice made him open his eyes. She was gazing toward the rock wall. When he turned and looked, the cave opening was there.

"How?" she asked.

Suddenly Dallas knew. He looked up at the sun directly overhead. "It's exactly noon," he said. "It was noon when we arrived yesterday. Noon when I rescued you the first time."

"We have to get you into the cave before the opening disappears again," Angel said.

"I'm not leaving you here alone."

"You don't have much choice," Angel said. "I belong here, Dallas."

He opened his mouth to argue with her and shut

it again. How could he say it was better for her in his world. He knew how it felt to be in the wrong place, in the wrong time. Could he really ask her to come with him to the future? Was it fair? Was it right? Especially when he wasn't sure exactly what his feelings were for her.

He was physically attracted to her. But what would happen when he tired of her? Or she tired of him? He couldn't bear the thought. Maybe she was right. Maybe he had to let her make her own choice.

"All right," he said. "I'll hold them off while you take the horse and escape."

"You can't—"

"Look, Angel. I'm not going at all if I have to leave you here with them. If you want me gone, you're going to have to make good your own escape. I'll pin them down and you make a run for it. When I'm sure you're safe, I'll head into the cave. They didn't have any luck following me last time, and I can lose them again just as easily."

Angel was torn. She didn't want him to go back to the future. But could she ask him to stay? This world wasn't anything like his own. He would likely regret his decision and leave her. And while she might be able to let him go now, she would never be able to do it later.

"All right," she said. "Be careful, Dallas, please. I'll...I'll miss you."

He didn't answer with words, just pulled her into his arms and kissed her hard, tasting, touching, gathering memories for the long years ahead. Abruptly, he released her.

"Go!"

Angel heard gunshots behind her as she kicked the mustang into a run. A bullet whined past her ear. Just before she reached a rise in the terrain—and safety—she turned the mustang and came galloping back toward Dallas.

She rode low on the pony, making as small a target as possible. She stopped the horse beside Dallas and said, "Grab hold of the horn and I'll help you get to the cave opening."

"Angel, damn you—"

"There isn't time to argue! Just do it!"

Grasping the stirrup, Dallas managed to get to his feet. He clung to the horn as Angel urged the mustang the short distance to the cave opening.

"They're gonna get away!" an outlaw cried.

"Not this time!" another answered. "I got enough dynamite to make sure they don't come outta there alive!"

Angel had only thought far enough ahead to realize that with his leg wound, Dallas needed her help getting to the cave entrance. But hearing the shouts from the outlaws made it clear that if she left him now, if she ran away to save herself, she was condemning Dallas to almost certain death. And that she could not do.

She didn't allow herself to contemplate the consequences of her actions. She dismounted and grabbed Dallas around the waist, helping him hobble into the cave.

"Angel, you have to leave," Dallas said in a weak voice. "Otherwise—"

"Shut up and keep walking," Angel said. "Neither one of us will have anything to complain about if we don't get away from the entrance to this cave."

They could hear the cowboys closing in on them. Dallas fired a warning shot to keep them at a distance, but they could hear from the cowboys' mutterings that they had other plans in mind.

"Got…to get…around that first bend," Dallas panted.

Angel could barely hold him up, he was so weak. "Come on, Dallas," she urged. "Just a little farther."

They had just turned the corner when they heard the explosion. Dallas staggered forward, dragging Angel along with him. This time the explosion didn't travel so far into the cave. Whether the walls were stronger, or the water had something to do with it, neither of them knew. But when the dust had settled, they were still alive.

"It's dark," Angel said into the silence.

Dallas pulled her close. "I know."

"I guess there's no going back now."

"I guess not."

"So, you're stuck with me," Angel said.

Dallas squeezed her hard. "Yeah. I guess I am."

7

Nearly thirty days had passed since they had returned from their journey to the past, and Angel
was still with Dallas.

Dallas had managed to drive the truck back to
his ranch and had called Adam Philips to the
house to treat his wound.

"Gun went off accidentally," Dallas explained
tersely when the doctor arrived.

Adam had looked at his friend askance, but he
hadn't questioned him. If he thought Angel's ravaged appearance in old-fashioned clothing odd, he
didn't mention it. "I'll have to report this gunshot
wound to the authorities," he said.

"Go ahead," Dallas said. "It was an accident." Dallas refused to go to the hospital. "Angel can take care of me at home," he said.

Adam clucked his tongue at his friend's stubbornness, but when Angel confirmed her willing-
ness to nurse Dallas, he didn't argue, just said,
"I'll be by to check on you regularly."

There was no investigation to speak of. Dallas

stuck by his story about how he'd been shot, and though Angel stood by white-faced, she didn't contradict him.

The Texas Rangers told Dallas to take his time getting back on his feet, but Dallas only managed to stay in his bed for about three days.

He had worried that his interference in the past might somehow have affected history. After all, he had killed several men who might have had important descendants. One of the first things he did was to search out the San Antonio newspaper dated October 7, 1864. He was intrigued by a portion of the article he found. It read:

A mysterious man claiming to be a Texas Ranger foiled an attempted jailbreak last night. After an all-night chase, the Texas Rangers captured the men responsible for blowing up the jail. The outlaws claimed that the man who shot convicted murderer and bank robber Jake Dillon said he was a Texas Ranger. The Rangers have no knowledge of the mystery man, whose name and whereabouts remain unknown.

Somehow, his intervention had become a part of history.

Satisfied that the past would remain the past,

Dallas had begun Angel's education in earnest. She was stuck in the future because she had saved his life. He was going to make sure she wasn't stuck with him—not if she didn't want to be, anyway.

Dallas had reminded Angel of the bargain they had made before they entered the cave for the last time—that she would learn what she needed to know to survive in the twentieth century. So far she hadn't balked at keeping it.

"I'm used to taking care of myself," she had said. "The sooner I'm able to be independent, the better."

Of course he had agreed with her. After all, didn't he value his privacy?

Dallas had been amazed at the way Angel threw herself into learning everything she could about the twentieth century. For the past few weeks he had been her teacher, and she had been—most of the time—an apt and willing pupil. Until today.

Dallas had saved driving lessons for last because he had feared that once Angel knew how to drive, she might steal his truck and disappear. Even now he didn't discount the possibility. However, first she had to learn to drive.

"Push down. Now let up. Easy does it. Give it some gas!" Dallas said.

The truck lurched and stalled. "I can't do it!" Angel cried. "I'll never get the hang of this!"

"You're doing fine," Dallas said. "Everybody has trouble learning to drive a stick shift at first."

"Did you?"

"Well, no, but—"

Angel shoved open the truck door and stepped down. "Who are you trying to fool, yourself or me? I don't fit in here," Angel ranted. "I can't do the simplest things."

Dallas slid across the seat and came after her. "Driving a stick shift isn't exactly simple."

"You can do it," she said scornfully over her shoulder.

"You aren't going to make me lose my temper, Angel, so stop trying."

She headed for Dallas's front porch and flopped down into a rocker there.

He followed her. "Over the past month you've learned how to use every appliance in the house," he said. "Even the computer."

Angel snorted. "I can turn it on and get words to appear on the screen. Anybody could do that."

"There you're wrong," Dallas said. "Lots of people are intimidated by computers. That's what makes you special, Angel. Nothing scares you off."

Angel stared at him in disbelief. If only he

knew! She had spent the past month terrified that she would find herself drowning in water over her head. Dallas had filled her as full of information as a mail-order catalog. If he hadn't been a patient man...

Even so, she had managed to provoke him often enough into losing his temper. It had become a sort of game—for her to push and him to shove back. The flare of tempers, his and hers, had helped to ease the sexual tension that was never far beneath the surface.

She threaded her fingers together and clutched them tight to keep from reaching out to Dallas. She wanted the comfort of being held in his arms. It wasn't a safe thing to ask for, because she was liable to get a whole lot more than comfort. Angel was inexperienced with men, but that didn't mean she was totally naive. She knew Dallas wanted her. Both his eyes and his body betrayed his desire. Since the day they'd returned from the past, he had been a perfect gentleman. She was going to do her darnedest to help him stay that way.

Dallas saw the muscles work in Angel's jaw and knew she had her teeth clenched again. It wasn't the first time and probably wouldn't be the last. The tension between them had gotten unbearable over the past month. He had tried to hide the way he felt about her, but being a man, his reaction had too often been visible.

He hadn't touched her. Not the way he'd wanted to, anyway. It was getting harder, though, not to reach out and hold her close, to fit them together as a man and woman were meant to be. Soon she would be independent. Soon she wouldn't need him at all, anymore. And, strange as it seemed, he felt a sense of impending loss.

"You can relax," Angel said. "I'm not going to burst into tears or have a hissy fit or start laughing hysterically. I've got myself under control."

"Sure you do," Dallas said, taking a seat on the top porch step. "You're some special kind of woman, Angel. Have I ever told you that?"

She rolled her eyes. "Once or twice a day for the past month."

He grinned. "Well, I mean it. You've got to cut yourself some slack. You can't expect to catch up on a hundred and twenty-odd years in thirty days."

Dallas always made a joke when he spoke about her coming from the past. Angel knew it was because he still didn't feel comfortable with the idea. But he also made her laugh when she felt like crying and provoked her into argument when she felt like giving up. She didn't know when she had ever met a man who challenged her the way he did.

The biggest surprise of all was that Dallas expected her to have a mind of her own and to use it. While Angel had never considered herself less capable than a man, she had never known a man who had treated her as an equal. Dallas's expectations were high, and it often took every ounce of courage she had to meet them. Like this driving business.

To be perfectly frank, the truck terrified her. Not that she hadn't driven a four-horse team in her day. She had. But there were *two hundred* horses under the hood of the truck. That was a lot of power. Dallas seemed to think she could handle it. She wasn't so sure.

Angel would have said forget it, except there were practical reasons why she had to overcome her fears. Dallas's leave of absence was up tomorrow, and if she didn't learn to drive, she would find herself isolated at his ranch. Not that she was looking forward to venturing out into the world without Dallas as a guide. The twentieth century was as daunting as it was exciting.

She had tried, over the past month, to find a place where she fit in. However, in this century, her lack of advanced education was a distinct disadvantage. Unfortunately, she hadn't much experience earning her living honestly, and Dallas had made it clear she wouldn't be earning it dishonestly.

Dallas had promised he would help her get whatever college degree she wanted, but the truth was, Angel had never been the best of students. She had spent more time in school daydreaming than studying. At Dallas's urging, she had agreed to sign up for some adult education courses at the local junior college. Which meant she had to learn how to drive so she could get to class.

Angel turned to Dallas, somewhat abashed by the childish tantrum her fears had caused. She huffed out a breath of air and said, "I'm sorry."

"I wish I had a tape recorder handy," he said. "I don't think those are words often heard from your lips."

"Tape recorder," Angel repeated. "That's the little box you talk into, and it repeats whatever you say back to you?"

"Yes. Or it can play music or other recordings."

"There's so much to remember!"

"You're doing fine," Dallas said, laying a hand on her knee. "Better than fine. Great."

"Except where driving is concerned."

"Want to give it another try?"

Angel shrugged nonchalantly. "Why not?" Everything had gone out of her head except an awareness of Dallas's hand on her knee. She subtly shifted out from under his hand, hoping he wouldn't notice.

Dallas noticed. His own response to the contact with Angel was seated a lot lower than her delightfully pinkened cheeks. The past month had been agony and ecstasy rolled into one. Having Angel living with him was like having a kid around—every experience was new and exciting for her. But she wasn't a kid, and his reaction to her was definitely a grown-up one.

Despite the moments of discomfort, he wouldn't have traded his time with her for anything. He desired her more than any woman he had ever known. Because he considered her vulnerable, he hadn't pressed her for a more intimate relationship. However, he found he couldn't leave her alone, either. Being her teacher had given him a good excuse to spend a lot of time with her.

He thought back over their first trip to a grocery store. Angel had picked everything up and examined it, looking for foods she recognized and inquisitive about those she didn't.

"Pineapple?" she had asked. "How can you eat something that's so prickly on the outside?"

"You cut the outside off," Dallas had explained. They'd bought one, and he'd had the pleasure of seeing her grin as the juice dripped down her chin.

Bread cut in slices, milk in a carton, fudge Popsicles, and of course more Twinkies and potato chips, quickly found their way into the shopping cart.

"This stuff is called spaghetti?"

"You'll love it," he had promised.

He had never laughed so much in his life as he did watching her twist spaghetti endlessly on a fork. She had laughed, too, once she got the hang of it.

Mexican food she knew, and insisted on buying all the ingredients for burritos, enchiladas and chili.

"I'm a pretty good cook with what I know," she'd said.

And she was. The stuff she cooked was so hot his head had nearly come off.

She knew all about tinned foods, which they'd had in 1864—not in such variety, of course. She'd reluctantly agreed to try the frozen ones, which he'd suggested were fresher tasting.

"Why these green beans look like they've just been snapped!" she exclaimed when she finally opened the package.

He'd felt as proud as though he'd personally planted the beans and hoed and harvested them.

Angel told him again and again how lucky he was to be able to walk up to the meat counter and have anything he wanted, not only skinned or plucked, but cut into serving sizes.

It had been a little touch and go at first when they got to the cosmetic and personal hygiene shelves at the grocery. Angel had wanted to know what everything was used for. In some cases his explanations were simple; in other cases they were not.

She was skeptical about using the makeup he pointed out to her. Only one kind of woman painted her face in 1864. Dallas had assured her that today it wasn't only the "soiled doves" who did. When he thought about it, he had found Angel's fresh face appealing without a hint of cosmetic aids. He pushed the cart right on by without suggesting that she purchase anything.

Explanations about some feminine products he knew she would need left them both red-faced by the time he finished. Angel put a box of the necessary items in the grocery cart with the comment, "These are really...convenient."

She picked up a box of condoms with the same eager innocence that had prompted each of her inquiries and read the label. Then she looked back up at the infinite variety of this particular product available. He watched her stiffen.

"What, exactly, is in this box?" she asked.

"A condom," he managed in what he thought was a creditably normal voice. "It…uh…a man wears it during… A man wears it." He felt unaccountably uncomfortable discussing it with her. Which was dumb. Everyone knew about condoms nowadays. He kept a box at home. They certainly didn't need to buy any more. However, he wanted her to understand what they were, how they were used and why. And he realized he'd been thinking a lot lately about what it would be like to make love to Angel. He'd better do this right.

"A man wears a condom during sexual intercourse," he explained.

He looked up and caught a very pregnant woman smiling at him from behind her shopping cart. He flushed to the roots of his hair. "Are you ready to go now?" he asked Angel.

"Not yet. It says here that a condom is 'highly effective against pregnancy.'"

"It's used for both contraception and protection from disease."

"Like syphilis?"

"Yes, and AIDS."

Her brow furrowed and he explained the devastation wrought in the past decade by the new disease. Meanwhile, syphilis was no longer the killer it had been in the past, but could be treated with medication.

It was plain from her distracted look that her thoughts were elsewhere. "You can actually prevent pregnancy with these?" she asked.

"A condom isn't a hundred percent effective," he said. "Pills are better for preventing pregnancy."

Her jaw dropped. "You have *pills* that keep a woman from having children?"

"It a choice some women make," he explained, keeping his voice low, aware that he still had an audience. "They take the pill until they're ready to start a family. Then they stop."

"You can actually *plan* when to have children?" she asked incredulously.

He grinned. "Sure can."

"I'll have to remember that," she murmured, a faraway look in her eyes. To his relief she had pushed the cart onward.

The subject of condoms hadn't come up again. The subject of intimacy between them hadn't come up, either. Not that *he* hadn't been up. Lots. In fact, he found himself in an almost perpetual state of arousal lately. All Angel had to do was turn those blue eyes of hers on him and he felt himself harden. If she touched his hand, his body responded instantly. Which was why he was glad his leave of absence was also finally up. He didn't know how much more of this close contact he could stand.

If he didn't get another thing accomplished today, he had to teach Angel how to drive. He needed her to be independent. And he knew she needed to be independent. She had chafed under the constraints placed on her by her ignorance of the twentieth century. She had learned more in a month than many people did in their lifetimes. And she had done it with guts and determination. He admired her more than any woman he had ever met.

Which was another reason he was glad to be going back to work. He liked having Angel around entirely too much. He had no use for a woman in his life. A woman couldn't be trusted to hang around for the long haul. Sooner or later Angel was going to start her wandering life again. The sooner she was out on her own, the better.

"Are you coming?" Angel called from the cab of the pickup.

"Coming," he replied as he headed for the passenger's seat. Once he was settled, he asked, "Do you want me to go through the instructions one more time?"

"No, I think I've got it. I just need to practice."

For the next half hour she did.

"It's a good thing this piece of Texas is so flat," she said at last, when she had mastered the basics.

"Once you get a little more practice, even hills won't be a challenge," he promised. "Do you feel comfortable enough to take a little drive?"

"Sure," Angel said. "Where shall we go?"

"How about if we drive over to visit Doc Philips?"

Adam Philips had dropped by several times over the past month to check on Dallas, but Angel had always retired to her room. Angel was not ordinarily a retiring sort of person, but the doctor was suspicious of the whole gunshooting episode, not to mention her quaint speech and her enthusiastic reactions to items that to others were perfectly ordinary. He had not given up trying to discover what was "wrong" with her.

Dallas had made very clear to her the danger of revealing the truth. People—like Adam Philips—would think she was crazy if she told them she was from the past. By the same token, she had to start being more social sometime. It looked like the end of Dallas's leave was going to mean the end of her hiatus from contact with other people.

"We don't have to go there, if you'd rather not," Dallas said, sensing her hesitancy.

"It's all right," she said. "It would be a good chance to practice driving. Maybe I ought to change my clothes first and put on a skirt."

"Your trousers are fine." He grinned. "A little baggy for my taste, but Adam won't notice."

Angel grimaced. "If you say so."

So far Angel had refused to wear anything that didn't cover her to the ankles. Dallas had vivid memories of what had happened when he took her shopping for clothes at the mall in San Antonio. He would never forget the shock on her face when she'd seen how the women were dressed. *He* had been embarrassed at some of the outfits, when he'd seen them through her eyes.

Bras worn as outerwear. Slinky, skin-tight, lace-edged pants worn as cutoffs. Short shorts that revealed sexy buttocks. Not that those things had ever bothered him before. It was hearing Angel's opinion that made him rethink the appropriateness of such garments in public.

"Those women aren't wearing enough clothes to dust a fiddle!" she hissed in his ear as she clutched at his elbow. "You're not going to suggest that I wear what they're wearing, are you?"

Actually, Dallas had been imagining what Angel would look like dressed up—or rather undressed—in twentieth-century fashions. "I'm sure we can find something more conservative for you," he said.

What he'd had in mind was a skirt that came to her knees. Angel, however, was having no part of that.

"You expect me to walk around exposing my limbs for any man who wants to gawk at them?" she asked, aghast. "I most certainly will not!"

At first Dallas had been angry at her inflexibility. "Everyone does it," he insisted.

"Not where I come from," she pointed out. "I would never feel comfortable dressed like that. A prairie dog knows his own hole, Dallas."

He gave up the fight when he realized that what he really wanted was to see her legs himself. It dawned on him that he wouldn't mind *at all* if no one else saw Angel's legs. He wasn't particularly proud of the feelings of possessiveness her attitude raised in him, but he didn't deny them, either. "All right," he said. "We'll just have to find something you do feel comfortable wearing."

They ended up in a country and western clothing store. There Angel found mid-calf-length cotton skirts and denim split riding skirts that, together with a pair of soft leather boots he bought her, conserved her modesty. They also found several lovely, very feminine blouses with western yokes to go along with the skirts.

Dallas had hesitated over whether to take Angel into the lingerie store in the mall, but he knew for a fact that she hadn't but one set of underwear. Having encountered resistance once, he took the time to explain to her what he was going to do.

"Women's undergarments have changed, Angel. I don't think we have the kind of thing you're used to wearing."

He saw her eyes go wide as she viewed all the undergarments displayed in the window of the store, for men and women alike to view. He felt her discomfort as his own and wished there was something he could do to make things easier for her. That was when he spied the saleswoman. He ushered Angel inside and walked right over to her.

"Can I help you sir, madam?" the woman asked.

"Uh…she needs some underthings," Dallas said.

"Do you have anything particular in mind?"

Angel blushed painfully.

"She needs a little of everything," Dallas said. "Bras, panties, slips…you know."

Fortunately the saleswoman was good at what she did and was used to male and female inhibitions around lingerie.

"Just let me take this young lady—what is your name?"

"Angel," Dallas said, when Angel remained mute.

"Angel, how lovely. Let me take Angel back and measure her, and we'll see what we can do."

Dallas had to admit that Angel looked miserable when she headed back into the dressing room with several lacy brassieres in hand.

When she came out, she admitted to Dallas, "It's a great improvement over a corset—not that I ever wore one much—but I feel dressed up like a sore wrist when I have one on. Isn't there anything that's more like what I'm used to wearing?"

The saleswoman looked at Dallas for further instructions. He matter-of-factly described for her what he had seen Angel wearing in his bathroom.

The saleswoman beamed and said, "I think I have just what you want."

The smile on Angel's face when she came out of the dressing room for the second time said it all. She was effusive in her praise of the undergarments the saleswoman had found for her. "They're so silky. And they feel wonderful next to my skin. As soft as Red's nose."

Dallas wanted to feel all those silky things for himself. Forget the silk. He was pretty sure her skin had Red's nose beat all to hell for softness.

He bought her several of the silk camisole tops and tap pants to match, which she found more familiar and less indecent than the bikini underwear the saleswoman had suggested.

After a short, pithy argument, Dallas had agreed to let Angel repay him for the cost of the clothes once she'd gotten a job. Both of them had been stymied about exactly what kind of work Angel could do. When he'd reminded her about taking some classes at the junior college, the subject of driving had come up.

"How will you get around if I have your truck?" Angel had asked.

"I have a car. After Cale was killed, one of the other Rangers brought me back here and I left it in San Antonio. I didn't need it, so I haven't picked it up. But I will when I go back to work."

Which he would have to do tomorrow. His captain had called him last night from San Antonio to give him another assignment. He had to be in Hondo in the morning. Some neighboring ranchers had been having a dispute over cattle that one claimed the other had rustled, and the local police had asked for the Texas Ranger's assistance in the investigation.

"Will you be coming home every day?" Angel had asked.

"It depends," he'd said. "If I'm working late,

maybe not.'' He had realized then that she *must* learn to drive.

Today, on the way to Doc Philips's, Dallas was hoping she would prove that she could. He had already covered her on his insurance policy and made sure she knew everything she would have been tested on had she gotten a license. The license itself would have to wait until he got her some identification.

''We can go the back way to Adam's place,'' Dallas said. ''It's a dirt road and doesn't get much traffic.''

Angel followed Dallas's directions to Adam's Lazy S Ranch without any trouble. She was grinning by the time she got there. ''I did it!''

''You sure did!'' Dallas opened his arms and Angel flung herself into them.

It really was the most innocent kind of hug, a sort of celebration of Angel's accomplishment. At least, that's the way it started. The instant Dallas felt Angel's soft breasts against his chest, he knew he was in trouble. His hands slid around her shoulders and up into her hair. Fingers tangled in silk. Blood pumped. Muscles tautened. Lungs heaved to suck air.

He murmured her name to feel his lips against her skin. He kissed her on the cheek, the nose, the eyes and finally found her mouth. All the hun-

ger, all the need that had been building for a
month was in that kiss.

Angel knew she was lost when his mouth found
hers. The need, the hunger, wasn't all on his side.
This time, when his tongue slid along her lips,
she opened her mouth. Then he was tasting her,
and she was kissing him back.

Dallas wanted more of their bodies touching,
but the stick shift was on the floor between them.
He had to half lift Angel to drag her across the
seat into his lap. To his great satisfaction, she
seemed both willing and eager to aid him in his
endeavor.

However, as Angel angled herself for better access, she ended up wedged against the truck horn.

A truck horn at a rural doctor's residence was
a sign of emergency. Those working on the Lazy
S responded accordingly. Cowhands came out of
the woodwork, the housekeeper left the kitchen,
and Doc Philips headed the horde as they all came
on the run.

The blare of the horn interrupted Dallas and
Angel long enough for Dallas to catch sight of
something moving out of the corner of his eye.
He pushed Angel away slightly to get a better
look, and they both watched in growing dismay
as the crowd converged on them.

"Let go!" Angel cried.

"I'm trying. Your hair is stuck in my shirt," Dallas retorted. "Move your leg."

"Not that way! Let go of my arm."

"Good grief! Straighten your blouse," Dallas said, helping her yank it back down to her waist. He looked down and groaned at the visible bulge in his trousers.

By then Adam had arrived at the driver's side of the pickup. "Are you two all right?" he asked breathlessly.

"Just fine," Angel answered in an equally breathless voice. She shoved a hand through her tangled hair.

Adam took one look at Angel's flushed face, her swollen lips and glazed, unfocused eyes and glanced at Dallas. Then he caught sight of Dallas's Stetson on his lap.

"We just came over so Angel could practice driving," Dallas said in a casual voice.

Adam's lips twitched in amusement. "I see you arrived all right." He grinned as he looked from Angel's mussed up hair to Dallas's flushed face. "In fact, it looks like you're both doing just fine. Would you like to come in and visit for a while?"

Dallas exchanged a quick look with Angel and saw the almost imperceptible shake of her head. "Uh, no," he said. "Thanks, anyway. Be seeing you."

Completely flustered, Angel managed to stall the truck twice before they got out of the driveway. The sound of laughter followed them down the road.

"I have never been so mortified in my life," she muttered.

"It's been a while since I was caught necking in the cab of a pickup myself," he muttered back.

Angel ground the gears as she shifted into third and hit the gas.

"Hey, slow down," Dallas said. "This road has a lot of—"

The truck hit a pothole that sent both of them flying. Angel lost control and the pickup ran off the road. Dallas grabbed the wheel and managed to keep them from hitting a large live oak tree. Between the two of them they brought the truck to a jarring stop.

"What bee got into your bonnet?" Dallas yelled. "You could have killed us both!"

Angel turned on him. "You flapdoodle chawbacon! You clunch! You know darned well what I'm upset about! If you would keep your hands to yourself and—"

"That tears it! I've had it!"

Angel mashed her lips flat and glared at him. Was he going to throw her out of the truck? Make her walk home?

"If you want someone courting you with words and keeping his distance, you're in the wrong time and place."

"And whose fault is that?" she accused.

"Look, Angel, men and women have a lot more freedom nowadays to explore their feelings outside of marriage. They—" Dallas thrust a hand through his hair.

"They what?" Angel asked, her whole body tensed.

"They do what comes naturally."

"Are you saying an unmarried woman can kiss...and touch...and even lie with a man, and nobody will think the worst of her."

Dallas trembled at the thought of Angel's mouth and hands on him, of the two of them lying naked together. "Yes."

"What if I want the courting words...and the respectful distance?" she asked soberly.

Dallas muttered an explicit four-letter word. She deserved the courting words and the respectful distance, didn't she? Was it her fault she'd been flung into a world where virginity until marriage was the exception, rather than the rule? But if that was the way she felt, she was sitting on a keg of dynamite living with him. Because he wasn't a marrying man, and he was having a helluva time keeping his distance.

He couldn't move her out into her own apartment; he'd spend too much time worrying about her. The only way he would feel comfortable was if he turned her over to someone else who cared about her welfare as much as he did. Suddenly he realized there was a way to solve both their problems—to give her a courting man and himself a little peace and quiet.

"What we need to do, Angel," he announced at last, "is find you a husband."

8

The piece of artists' charcoal in Angel's hand moved almost with a will of its own over the paper before her. The junior college art instructor, Mr. Collinsworth, had said, "Choose a subject to draw that's close to you, something you've seen or done." Over the past three weeks of classes, Angel had done a series of drawings. The latest was a sketch of Belinda as she had appeared the last time Angel had seen her.

The woman taking shape in charcoal looked hard, her eyes disillusioned, her mouth flattened by disappointment, her chin thrust in defiance. Yet it was apparent she was physically young, her skin soft, her lashes long and frilled, her face a sweet, nicely shaped heart. Her hair was coiled up primly on top of her head, but lush tendrils dripped from her temples.

Her striped silk and taffeta dress was straight from the latest *Godey's Lady's Book,* but the breasts beneath the fabric strained for freedom. Though you couldn't tell it in charcoal, Angel remembered the dress had been a deep red with tiny black pin stripes. The woman held a delicate parasol across her shoulder, with black fringe that the wind moved in a ripple, like a wave. Belinda's fingerless mesh glove revealed broken and ragged fingernails.

In the background Angel had drawn the exterior of the seedy-looking house where Belinda worked. Where she had met Jake Dillon. Where she had spent the last days of her life.

It was a portrait of opposites: youth and age, constraint and abandonment, propriety and a prostitute. That's what Angel mentally named the drawing when she was done.

She was aware of the teacher standing behind her, observing her finished sketch on the easel. Angel had done a lot of pencil sketches to fill her spare time as she wandered across Texas, but she had shown them to no one. It was hard to let the teacher see what she had done, because Angel always put a part of herself on paper.

She fidgeted nervously as Mr. Collinsworth continued his silent examination of the drawing.

At last he said, ''I'm not sure exactly what I'm going to be able to teach you in this drawing class, Ms. Taylor. You seem to have an extraordinary grasp of composition and texture, and especially of light and shadow. Once again, your work leaps right off the page, as though you were actually there with this woman in the nineteenth century.''

That's because I was! Angel thought. ''Thank you, Mr. Collinsworth,'' she said.

''Have you ever exhibited any of your work?''

Everything Angel had ever drawn had been ruined along with her rucksack. She simply answered, ''No.''

''Would you like to? If you can do pen and ink drawings like this, I know a gallery in Houston that might be interested in presenting a collection of your work.''

Angel smiled, unaware of the effect her shining eyes were having on Mr. Collinsworth. ''Thank you. I would appreciate that.''

''Fine. We'll go get a cup of coffee after class tonight and plan your future—artistically speaking, of course,'' he added with a teasing wink.

Angel found his forwardness a contrast to the almost shy, respectful way a man in the past would have treated a respectable woman. However, seeing as how she was supposedly in the market for a husband, having coffee would allow her to give Mr. Collinsworth a good looking over.

Not that she really intended to marry anybody. She was just humoring Dallas. He had told her at breakfast that if she didn't start choosing some men on her own, *he* would pick the gents to court her.

That had started another argument between them, which she had won when Dallas had to abandon the field to go to work. He had promised—threatened—to pick up where he'd left off when he got home that evening.

The problem was that of all the men Angel had ever met, past and present, Dallas was the one who fit her image of a man worth marrying. Whenever she got near him she felt tense and excited. Maybe it was the fact he was a Texas Ranger, a breed of men known as much for their ruthlessness as for their sense of honor. The heck of it was, she didn't want to be attracted to Dallas. He had sworn over eggs and toast that he wasn't the marrying kind.

So maybe having a cup of coffee with Mr. Collinsworth wasn't such a bad idea after all.

Dallas rubbed the back of his neck, trying to ease the tension. The rustling investigation in Hondo was complicated by the fact that one of the local lawmen was related to one of the complaining parties. That's where the Texas Rangers usually came in. Their reputation was above reproach.

Dallas realized to his chagrin that he was looking forward to coming home, not so he could be alone, but because Angel was there. During the past three weeks since he had gone back to work, this new attitude had crept up on him. If he didn't do something soon to get Angel out of his house and out of his life, he was afraid he would end up asking her to stay forever.

His lips curled cynically. Not that there was any such thing as *forever* with a woman. Dallas wondered whether it might not be worth the heartache down the road to have a woman like Angel for a wife. Then he remembered the gray pallor of his father's face after reading the Dear John letter from his mother, and he sobered. There was no sense fooling himself. No woman was worth enduring that kind of pain.

He had reconsidered the idea of setting Angel up in an apartment, but realized there were too many pitfalls for her living in the unfamiliar future. Besides, he wanted to make sure some scoundrel didn't take advantage of her naiveté. She deserved his protection until another man came along to take over the job. Not that Angel appreciated his consideration. She had told him in no uncertain terms, that she could take care of herself! Sometimes she sounded an awful lot like a twentieth-century woman.

Nonetheless, Dallas had racked his brain trying

to think of men with whom he could pair Angel and had come up with only a few choices. Adam Philips was one of them. Dallas planned to approach Adam tonight on the way home to see whether the good doctor might be interested in getting to know Angel Taylor a little better.

As Dallas drove over the cattle guard onto Lazy S property, he tugged his Stetson down to shadow his worried eyes. With his mouth set in a firm line, he pulled his pickup—Angel had his car—up to the front of the U-shaped adobe house.

Adam looked surprised to see him, as well he should. Dallas didn't usually go visiting without an invitation.

"What can I do for you?" Adam said as he held the screen door so Dallas could come in. "Is Angel all right?"

Dallas cleared his throat and thrust his hands in the back pockets of his jeans. "She's fine. But she's what brought me here."

"Have a seat. I'll get you a drink." Adam went to a bar in one corner of the living room and poured Dallas a short shot of whiskey, straight up. He poured himself a brandy. When they were both settled in two heavy Mediterranean chairs facing the crackling fire in a stone fireplace, Adam asked, "Want to tell me what this is all about?"

Dallas took a sip of whiskey and waited for it

to warm his insides. He rested his forearms on his thighs and stared into the licking flames. That's what Angel did to him, licked at his insides like flame that was going to burn him up if he didn't escape. He rubbed the whiskey glass with his thumbs, took a drink and said, "I was wondering if you might be interested in getting to know Angel Taylor a little better."

"Sure," Adam said. "Why don't you two come over for dinner on Sunday and—"

"No." Dallas leaned back in the massive chair and crossed one boot over the other knee. A flush burned its way up his neck, and he took another sip of whiskey—as if that was going to ease his discomfort. There was nothing to do but blurt it out. "I meant, would you be interested in dating Angel?"

Adam obviously was caught off guard. "She's certainly a beautiful woman, but..."

"But?" Dallas said aggressively.

"I thought you wanted her for yourself."

Dallas grimaced. "Not hardly. Although I do feel responsible for her. I wouldn't want you taking advantage of her."

Adam quirked a brow. "Would that by any chance include not sleeping with her?"

"You're damned right, it would! Angel isn't

like that. Besides, she'd probably cut your heart out if you tried,'' Dallas added with a boyish grin.

''What's the catch?'' Adam asked.

''No catch.''

''Then why don't you want her for yourself?''

''Angel's the marrying kind,'' Dallas said, as though that explained everything. And because Adam knew about his mother, it did.

Adam pondered for a moment before he said, ''I have to admit I find her attractive. Sure. Why not?''

''When?''

''I'll think about it and give Angel a call,'' Adam said pointedly.

Dallas knew he was being told to butt out. He had opened the door, now he had to get out of the way so Adam could come on through it. He rose and set the empty whiskey glass on a nearby table. ''I'll be seeing you.''

Adam nodded goodbye as Dallas let himself out.

Dallas had done what he had to do, but he didn't feel good about it. By the time he got home, he felt sick to his stomach. His agitation got worse when he discovered the house was dark. Angel should have been home from class an hour ago. Where was she?

As he let himself into the empty house, he realized how lonely it felt. He had never noticed the loneliness before. The place was so quiet. There were signs everywhere of Angel's absence.

She wasn't the neatest roommate he'd ever had.

An unfinished Monopoly game was spread out on the trestle table. The sweatshirt she had worn last night was draped across the sofa. Copies of every women's magazine she could find were interspersed with his men's magazines across the hardwood floor.

His whole house smelled like her.

He identified the lingering scent of the perfume she wore. It was a dark, musky scent, heavier that he would have expected her to choose. Perhaps she had chosen it specifically because it was stronger, more earthy, more primitive. He felt his body tighten. She was getting to him, and she wasn't even here!

She disliked using modern mechanical devices.

Dallas went to the phone answering machine to see if she had left him a message. There was a call from the lawman in Hondo asking him to come early on Monday morning and join him for breakfast, but nothing from Angel. What was keeping her? He was beginning to get concerned.

But there was nothing wrong with her appreciation of the variety of foods available.

He went into the kitchen and opened the refrigerator, but realized he wasn't hungry—not for food, anyway. Signs of Angel were there, too. The more exotic something was, the more she liked it. So he found cranberry instead of orange juice, papayas instead of apples.

She liked modern country music; it reminded her of the past.

He wandered into the living room and turned on the radio. A Willie Nelson tune, something woeful about a woman leaving her man, only made him more anxious.

She said she didn't intend to date anybody, but what if she had changed her mind? What if she was with some other man right now?

"You're being ridiculous," he told himself. "There are a dozen good reasons why she could be late getting home. Stop worrying like a hen with one chick!"

He pulled the snaps free on his white-yoked western shirt, intending to take a shower. He had already started the water running when he realized there were also a dozen things that could have gone wrong. Angel might have had a flat tire. Of course he'd taught her how to change it, but what if she forgot something? What if she had run out of gas? What if she'd had engine trouble?

None of those possibilities were probable. Probably class had just run late. Dallas wasn't thinking like a rational man. The next "what ifs" that crossed his mind had him shutting off the water and retrieving his shirt from the bathroom rack where he'd flung it.

What if she had decided to go out for a drink with someone after class? She had no idea how fast the modern American male moved in on a woman. She was a lamb in a den of wolves. He had to find her!

Her car wasn't stalled anywhere on the road between the junior college and home. He knew class wasn't running late, because the art building was black as Hades. That meant she must have gone somewhere—with some man?—after class.

Dallas ran through the likely places to get an alcoholic drink in Uvalde. There weren't many. He checked them all and came up blank. Maybe by now she had gone home. He drove to the nearest phone, called home...and got the answering machine.

Coffee. That's where she'd gone. To get a cup of coffee. He checked the most likely location, a motel with a café right on the main drag into town.

He found his car in the parking lot.

Dallas walked into the Bluebird Café as though he had just stopped by on his way home from Hondo for a cup of coffee and a piece of buttermilk pie. He let the waitress, Mary Jo Williams, seat him by the window in front and pour his coffee. Angel was sitting at the rear of the café with a man whose back was to Dallas, but whom he had already identified as Ray Collinsworth.

Angel saw Dallas the moment he came in and knew he had seen her, as well. Why hadn't he come back to greet her? Why was he sitting by the window, pretending she didn't exist?

"So my wife and I decided to get a divorce," Ray Collinsworth said.

Angel knew from reading how prevalent divorce was in the late 1900s, but it still shocked her. "Wasn't there any way you could work out your problems?"

He shrugged. "Bobbie Sue wanted to live in the big city. Uvalde's growing, but it's still a small town compared to Dallas."

"Why didn't you just go with her?" Angel asked.

"My roots are here. So's my family. There's nothing in Dallas I want."

"Except Bobbie Sue," Angel said.

"Yeah, well, she's history now," Ray said. "I want to move on with my life. Start dating again. Which is one of the reasons I asked you to have coffee with me. I admire your talent, Angel. Whatever does or doesn't happen between us, I'll do whatever I can to make sure you get a gallery showing in Houston. But I'd like to see you outside of class, if you'd be interested.''

"She wouldn't."

Ray Collinsworth looked over his shoulder and froze at the forbidding sight that greeted him. "What are you doing here, Dallas?"

"Angel lives with me."

Ray swallowed hard. "I didn't know."

"Now you do."

"I was just leaving," Ray said. "Good night, Angel, uh, Ms. Taylor." He grabbed the check and started to edge past Dallas.

Dallas took the check from between Ray's fingers. "I take care of Angel."

Ray gulped, nodded and fled.

The instant the other man was gone, Dallas slid into the booth across from Angel.

Angel had watched Dallas's performance with astonishment first and then with growing anger. "Nobody takes care of me, Ranger," she said in a voice that shook. "I take care of myself!"

"I could see how well you were taking care of yourself," Dallas retorted. "Another second and Ray Collinsworth would have had you agreeing to anything he suggested—and we both know what he'd suggest."

"That's my choice to make," she insisted. "Not yours."

"Ray's wife left him with three kids," Dallas said. "He's spent the past year looking for someone to be a mother for them."

"He told me about his children. They sounded delightful."

Dallas snorted. "Yeah. Delightful little monsters."

"Children are what you expect them to be," she said.

"Are you speaking with the voice of experience?"

"Belinda had a daughter, Penny. Before Penny died of pneumonia, I used to take care of her when Belinda was…busy. Children don't ask for much. And we give them too little."

"If you like kids so much, maybe I can talk you into going with me tomorrow to visit Cale's widow and his two sons."

Dallas didn't hear the anguish in his voice when he mentioned Cale's family. Angel did. There could be no question of her response. "I'll be glad to go with you. Do they live nearby?"

"Cale's ranch is south of Uvalde. It's been in his family for generations. His wife, Honey, is having a hard time holding things together. I thought I'd go by and see if there's anything I can do to help out.''

"What time do we leave?"

"Early. We'd best be getting home. I'll follow you."

"What if I'm not ready to leave?" Angel said, irked that he was ordering her around again.

"I'll wait until you are," he said flatly.

Angel made a face. "Of all the hickory-headed—"

"Sticks and stones may break my bones, but names—"

Angel laughed. "All right. Let's go!" As she rose, Dallas put a hand under her elbow to lead her out of the cafe. Even that little touch was enough to sensitize her to his presence—and remind her that while he might want her in bed, he didn't want any kind of permanent relationship with her.

When they reached the register, she slipped the check out of his hand and said, "I'll pay."

"But—"

She raised a brow and said, "Do you, or don't you want me to be a twentieth-century woman?"

"Pay the check," he said.

Dallas shook his head at the smug look on Angel's face as she pulled the necessary money out of her pocket—money she'd won from him playing poker—and slapped it on the counter. She didn't wait for him, simply got into his car and took off toward home.

By the time he parked his pickup in the driveway and got inside the house, she was already in her bedroom.

"What time should I set my alarm?" Angel called to him through the door.

"How about 7:00 a.m.?"

"Fine. I—"

The jarring ring of the phone interrupted Angel. She let Dallas answer it, since no one she knew would be calling her.

"It's for you," he said a second later. "Adam Philips."

Now that Adam had called, Dallas was having all kinds of second thoughts. Maybe he was making a mistake trying to rush Angel into a relationship. Maybe he ought to let things happen in their own good time. He recognized the source of his problem when Angel stepped out of his bedroom wearing one of the shapeless T-shirts he'd bought for her. Jealousy. In fact, he was feeling green as buffalo grass.

"Here." He thrust the phone into her hands, anxious to be away from her before he did something he would regret. Like hanging up the damned phone and pulling her into his arms and kissing her the way he'd been wanting to for the past two hours since he'd first seen her sitting across from Ray Collinsworth.

Angel had no idea why Dallas was so upset. She took the phone, expecting some sort of bad news. "Hello?"

"Hi, Angel," Adam said. He laughed. "That has a nice sound to it. Hi, Angel," he said again. "I wondered if you'd like to go tubing on the Frio River with me tomorrow?"

"Tomorrow?" She looked up and saw Dallas glaring at her from the kitchen. "I'm afraid not. I have plans tomorrow."

"How about Sunday, then?"

"Sunday would be fine. What time?"

"I'll pick you up about nine. I'll bring a picnic and we'll make a day of it. See you Sunday."

Angel held the phone to her ear for a moment before she hung up. "Adam wants to take me tubing on the Frio."

"I heard."

"I'm going."

"I heard."

"You don't have any objections?"

"Adam Philips is a fine man. You could do worse."

"I wonder why he suddenly called up out of the blue like that?"

"I wouldn't know," Dallas said.

The look on his face said otherwise. "Did you say anything to Adam about asking me out?" she asked in a calm, controlled voice.

"What if I did? You weren't making any progress meeting men on your own."

Angel was outraged. "How could you? What if I hadn't wanted to go out with Adam Philips?"

"You would have told him so."

"Since I said yes, is there any advice you'd like to give me before I go out with him?"

Don't kiss him. Don't touch him. Don't let him touch you! "No."

9

Despite what Dallas had said about kids being monsters, he seemed to be enjoying himself with Jack and Jonathan Farrell. From where Angel stood in the vegetable garden behind the Farrell house, she could see that all three had their shirts off and were working to repair the corral together. Seven-year-old Jonathan barely reached Dallas's waist. Twelve-year-old Jack had sprouted high enough to reach the Ranger's shoulders.

Pictured before Angel were a rib-thin child, a gangling youth and a mature man. The child made her long for one of her own; the youth reminded her of a fledgling bird, not quite ready to leave the nest. And the man made her throat go dry as she imagined herself enfolded in the strength revealed by his muscular torso, with its pelt of black hair arrowing down into his jeans. She wished she could stop hoeing long enough to preserve the scene on paper.

"They look good together, don't they?"

Angel started and looked at Honey Farrell, who

was hoeing weeds one row over from her. "Yes, they do."

Honey wiped her brow with a bandanna, then stuck it in the back pocket of her short, cutoff jeans and started working again. "The boys miss Cale. The four of them—Cale, Dallas, Jack, and Jonathan—used to spend the day together sometimes, working on the ranch like this. I remember one time—"

Angel looked up to see why Honey had stopped speaking and saw the woman standing frozen, her throat working to hold back sobs, her eyes brimmed with tears. Angel's first impulse was to leap over the row of lettuce and comfort Honey. Before she could act, however, the young woman had smeared the tears away with her shirtsleeve and was viciously hoeing the ground again.

"I asked Cale to quit the Rangers," she said angrily. "Do you know what he told me?"

It was a rhetorical question. Honey didn't pause long enough for Angel to answer.

"He told me that being a Texas Ranger made him feel alive—that it constantly tested his courage. Rangers are different, you know, from ordinary men. Most of them aren't just brave—they don't know what fear is. Cale loved danger. If it hadn't been a constant part of his job, he would have sought it somewhere else. I told him his work was too chancy, that I couldn't bear to lose him. I even threatened to leave him once."

She paused and sighed. "I never could have done it. I loved him and he knew it. He promised to be careful. I know he tried, but sometimes... sometimes he was too impetuous, too impatient for his own good. It cost him his life."

Angel had never considered the dangers Dallas faced as a Texas Ranger. In the world she had come from, violence and death were an inescapable part of life. In this century, men could choose to live peacefully, without a gun at hand. Yet Dallas had risked his life without a qualm to rescue her at the cave. He had responded with cold, calculating action to the biker who threatened her. She realized suddenly that his boldness, his fearlessness, were part of what made him attractive to her. She recognized Dallas as a man who could have survived in her world as capably as he did in his own.

Honey ended the thoughtful silence between them by saying, "Jack worshipped his father. He wants to be a Texas Ranger like his dad."

"Have you tried talking him out of it?" Angel asked.

"*Yes, I have,*" Honey said emphatically, punctuating her words with stabs at the earth. She smiled bitterly. "A lot of good it's done me. Jack has inherited some of his father's stubbornness."

Honey had reached the end of her row. "Shall we take a break and make iced tea for everybody?"

"I have another couple of feet to go to finish this row. I'll join you in a few minutes," Angel said.

Angel took advantage of the opportunity to watch Dallas at work. The three males were pulling out a rotting corral post, and Angel watched the ropey muscles bunch in Dallas's shoulders as he strained to break the post free. His skin was shiny with sweat, and beads of moisture clung like crystals to the hair on his chest.

Dallas had tied a bandanna around his forehead to keep the moisture out of his eyes; the smaller boy had copied him and looked adorable. When the post finally came free, Dallas ruffled Jonathan's hair. The older boy, Jack, shied away from Dallas's congratulatory slap on the shoulder and slanted a look—of loathing?—at the Ranger.

Honey was already on her way to the corral with a tray of iced tea by the time Angel finished hoeing. She took a second to lean on the hoe and watch as Dallas slipped his shirt on, the sort of courtesy she might have expected from a gentleman in her day. She didn't miss the way Dallas gave Honey's legs a quick once-over. Honey's shirt was tied in a knot at the waist in front, emphasizing her breasts. All in all, Angel had to admit the woman was a feast for male eyes.

What surprised her was that on Honey the exposed skin didn't look lurid, it looked natural. To be honest, although Dallas looked at and enjoyed the view, he didn't treat Honey any less respectfully because of the way she was dressed. Angel realized she might have to revise her opinion of women who dressed in scanty clothing.

The two boys quickly gulped down their iced tea and wandered off toward the barn. Angel watched Dallas's face as Honey followed the progress of her sons and saw the concern there. He had told Angel he felt responsible for Cale's family. Would he consider taking Cale's place? Marrying Honey? Being a father to Cale's sons?

Angel dropped the hoe and headed for the corral. As she approached, she heard Honey say, "You don't know how much I appreciate your help, Dallas. I would have gotten to that post eventually, but it was threatening to collapse any day."

"I only wish you'd let me do more," he answered.

"You've got your own life," Honey said. "We'll manage."

"Cale asked me to—"

"Cale is dead." Honey's voice was brittle with pain. She took a deep breath, searching for and finding control of her tumultuous emotions. "You've been a good friend, Dallas. You don't owe Cale—or us—any more than that."

She turned and was gone before Dallas or Angel could say a word to stop her.

"She's right, you know."

Dallas turned to look at Angel over his shoulder. "I'm not so sure."

Angel climbed up and sat facing Dallas on the top rail of a sturdy section of the corral. "She has to carve out a new life for herself that doesn't include her man. The more you help, the less likely she is to shoulder the burden herself. The sooner she does, the better for her and her sons."

"It's too much for her," Dallas said flatly.

"I think you're underestimating her," Angel said. "She'll manage."

"Through good old self-sufficiency and self-reliance, huh?"

Angel shrugged. "I saw a lot of women lose their husbands to violent, premature deaths in the War Between the States. It was either crawl into the grave with them or keep on living. Most of them chose to keep on living. I'd say Honey has, too."

Dallas rubbed at the wrinkles of concern on his brow. "I feel so responsible somehow. Those boys of hers—they need a father."

"Are you volunteering for the job?" Angel could have bitten off her tongue. Why put ideas into his head?

"I've thought about it," he admitted.

"What's stopping you?"

"For one thing, Honey isn't about to let another Texas Ranger into her life."

Angel pursed her lips. "I think I have to agree with you there. Maybe the best thing is to be a friend, like she asked."

Excited cries from the two boys in the barn interrupted their conversation.

"Sounds like a small riot going on in there," Angel said.

"I'd better go check on them."

Angel tagged along. She was stunned when she entered the barn with Dallas to see the two boys fighting on the straw-covered floor. Arms and legs were tangled, teeth were bared, hands were fisted. Angel stepped back out of the way as Dallas grabbed hold of one boy with each hand and yanked them to their feet. He held them at arm's distance from each other, so their fists and feet flailed ineffectually.

"Settle down," Dallas said in a steely voice.

The two boys immediately dropped their fists and stood glaring at each other, sullen and defiant.

"What's this all about?" he demanded.

"He started it," the older boy said.

The younger one retorted, "Jack said Dad was stupid! He said Dad got himself killed trying to be a hero!"

Dallas's face blanched. "Your father saved my life," he said. "It cost him his own. That doesn't make him any more or less than what he was—a brave man who saw his duty and did it."

By now Angel saw that the older boy was hanging his head. The younger one was looking up at Dallas and asked, "Were you there when my dad died?"

"Yes."

"Did he say anything to you about me and Jack before he...uh...died?"

Dallas released both boys and knelt down in front of Jonathan. Angel noticed that although Jack's head was still down, his eyes were focused on Dallas.

Dallas straightened the younger boy's shirt, feeling the need for some sort of physical contact with him. "Your father said he loved you both," Dallas said. "He asked me to come see you when I could. He said he knew you would take care of your mother and be a help to her. He hoped you would grow up to be good men.''

''He should have saved himself,'' Jack blurted. ''You should have been the one to die!''

Dallas rose and faced Jack, man to man. ''I've thought the same thing,'' he admitted quietly. ''Your father could have saved himself. He could have let me die. I know he must have considered the risk—that he might not be coming back to you boys and your mother. But you knew your dad, Jack. Could he have lived with himself if he hadn't tried his best to save me?''

Angel watched Jack swallow over a painful knot in his throat. The twelve-year-old boy's mouth opened, then closed. He clenched his jaws and it was clear he was fighting unmanly tears.

At last he lifted his eyes and met Dallas's gaze. ''I...I'm sorry for what I said to you just now.''

Dallas laid a hand on Jack's shoulder, and though the boy flinched, he didn't jerk away. ''Your father was a man to be proud of,'' Dallas said. ''I owe him my life. If you ever need me for anything, anything at all, I want you to call me. Do you understand?''

Jack nodded.

''Does that go for me, too?'' Jonathan piped up.

Dallas laid a hand on Jonathan's shoulder as

well. "That definitely goes for you, too. Now, how about if we get back to work?"

Dallas led the two boys past Angel, a hand on each of their shoulders. He was talking earnestly to Jack about what ranch jobs the boy could manage on his own over the upcoming summer vacation and what he would need help doing. Meanwhile Jonathan wanted Dallas to help him choose a horse to buy for his very own.

"Mom wants me to get a pony, but Dad said I could get a *horse*. Don't you think I ought to have a *horse*, Dallas?"

Angel took her time getting to the house. It was clear there was a lot more to Dallas Masterson than met the eye. He hadn't pulled any punches with the two youths. He had told them the truth— that their father had died saving another man's life. But he also had made it clear that their father had done the right thing—the only thing he could do and still look himself in the mirror. He had shown them that their father's sacrifice was appreciated. If they needed help, Dallas was there for them.

Angel wished her own children could have a father like Dallas. She imagined what her children—with Dallas as their father—might look like. The boys would be tall and brown-haired like their father; the girls would be tall, too, but with blond hair like hers. She pictured them sitting gathered around the porch of Dallas's Victorian home—

Suddenly Angel realized that she wanted the picture she was sketching in her mind to be real. The never-admitted longing she had felt for a hearth and home of her own had crystalized in one man. The truth hit her in the face like a mule kick.

She was in love with Dallas Masterson!

Angel didn't remember much about the rest of the day with the Farrell family. She had been lost in a fog of euphoria over her revelation. She spent the day planning ways to convince Dallas that they belonged together and that she would make him a good wife. It was at dusk, as they were leaving, that her imaginary bubble burst.

Honey and her two sons had come outside to the truck to bid her and Dallas farewell. She couldn't believe her ears when she heard Dallas say, "You're sure you don't want me to come by tomorrow morning and pick you up?"

"No. The boys and I will be at your place to go tubing by nine sharp. Never fear. And thanks, Dallas. I didn't realize until you suggested it just how much we need to get away from the ranch for a day."

"See you tomorrow morning, then," he said. With a smile and a wave he started the truck and headed down the drive.

Angel was shocked. And dismayed. Had Dallas reconsidered the possibility of courting Honey Farrell? Was this tubing trip intended to change her mind about getting involved with another Texas Ranger?

"When did you decide to ask Honey to go tubing?"

"After supper, while you were drawing with the kids." *And looking like one yourself.*

Dallas had taken one look at Angel lying sprawled unself-consciously on the living room floor, her chin supported on one palm, her lips curved in an amused smile as her pencil moved a mile a minute creating caricatures of Jack and Jonathan, and realized there was no way he was letting her go off alone with Adam Philips.

"Did you invite Honey to come tubing so you can come along and keep an eye on me?" she asked suspiciously.

"No," he denied.

The flush on his cheeks gave him away. And gave Angel hope. If he didn't want her alone with Adam Philips, it might mean he cared about her. On the other hand there was no telling what might happen with Honey along. More than one man had lost his heart to a woman without intending to.

Honey wasn't just pretty, she was gorgeous, with dazzling, honey-blond hair, bright blue eyes and a flawless complexion. Not only was she pretty, she had a figure out of a man's dreams. Honey was a tall woman; her body would accommodate Dallas's lanky frame a lot better than Angel's petite size did.

Angel thought back to the few times Dallas had embraced her. He invariably had had to pick her up to fit them together in all the right places. Of course, in a prone position respective heights wouldn't be a problem. But Angel couldn't very well point that out to Dallas without getting into a prone position with him. And that was unlikely at best, considering the current state of affairs.

Angel had actually considered canceling the date with Adam when she realized she was in love with Dallas. Now, not only was she going on the date, she had to wear something that would keep Dallas's eyes on her instead of Honey Farrell. Which meant she was, at last, going to have to expose her limbs like a twentieth-century woman.

By the time they arrived back at Dallas's house, Angel was gnawing at her lower lip, anxious about the step she had decided to take.

"What's wrong?" Dallas asked.

"I can't decide what to wear tomorrow."

Dallas smiled. From all the fidgeting she'd been doing for the past hour, he'd expected it to be something serious. "That doesn't sound like such a problem."

Annoyed, she met his amused gaze and said, "I was thinking maybe I ought to make some cutoffs out of a pair of my jeans. What do you think?"

Maybe this was serious after all.

"I thought you'd already decided you don't have to conform to modern dress codes," Dallas said.

"That's true. But if I'm going to be spending the entire day in the water, wearing something that covers me to the ankles doesn't make much sense."

"It makes more sense than going naked!" Dallas snapped.

"I wasn't planning on stripping to the skin," Angel replied in a voice Dallas found irritatingly calm. "I just thought I'd cut off a pair of my jeans."

"How high are you planning to cut?" Would Adam end up ogling her knees? Her thighs? The curve of her enticing bottom?

"I don't know," Angel said. "I thought I'd start at the knee, and—" She shrugged. "I'll just have to see how high I can go and still feel comfortable.''

''I think you're making a mistake.''

''We'll find out, won't we? Do you have a pair of scissors?''

Dallas marched into the kitchen and pulled open a utensil drawer. He stomped back out again and handed her the scissors. ''Here. I hope you know what you're doing.''

Angel grinned. ''I hope so, too.''

Dallas spent the night staring at the ceiling and wondering what was wrong with him. He didn't care a fig that Adam was probably going to see Honey Farrell in a bikini. But he couldn't stand the thought of Angel's knees on display. He was crazy. Certifiable. Angel had finally sent him over the bend.

The next morning Dallas was so tired he felt hung over. Angel was full of vim and vinegar. In fact, she hadn't stopped talking since she'd stepped out of her bedroom dressed in a T-shirt, cutoffs and white canvas tennis shoes without socks.

Dallas took a long look at her cutoffs. Mid-thigh. Not as good as he'd hoped (down to her knees). Nor as bad as he'd feared (exposing her rear end). It dawned on him that there was something unbelievably erotic about looking at a woman's ankles, calves and knees, when you knew no other man had ever seen them before. It was like eating of forbidden fruit. More delicious because it was taboo.

He cleared his throat and said, "You have beautiful legs."

"Thank you." Pink tinged Angel's cheeks. She couldn't help feeling a little self-conscious, even though her cutoffs were considerably more modest than the shorts Honey had been wearing the previous day. At the same time she felt a sense of freedom and adventure.

"Hey! Anybody home?" Adam let himself in the kitchen door. He stopped short when he saw Angel. "What have we here? Venus in blue jeans."

"Cutoff blue jeans," Dallas corrected. "How would you feel about having some company today?"

Adam slipped an arm around Angel's shoulder and grinned at Dallas. "Frankly this is a trip I'd rather make alone."

A honking horn kept Dallas from saying something to Adam that he would have regretted later.

"Expecting company?" Adam asked.

"Cale's widow and her two sons," Dallas said. "Figured we'd all go tubing together."

Adam was aghast. "All of us? A widow, two kids, you, me and Angel?"

Dallas's smile was slow coming, but it was smug when it got there. "Yeah."

"Dallas? Are you in there?" Honey pushed his screen door open and stuck her head inside. When she spied Dallas, the rest of her—and almost all of her was visible in the sapphire-blue French cut bikini—slowly materialized.

Dallas watched with wicked glee as Adam's jaw dropped. The good doctor was positively drooling. Well, so much for distraction. While the doc was pursuing the luscious woman in the bikini, Dallas would entertain himself with a female who had been daring enough to expose her ankles, calves and knees to public view for the first time.

"Everybody ready?" Dallas asked.

Jack and Jonathan shouted their enthusiasm. Honey glanced shyly at Adam. Adam cleared his throat. Angel tugged on the hem of her cutoffs.

Dallas grinned. "Then, let's go!"

10

It wasn't hard for Dallas to manipulate things so Adam ended up tubing with Honey, while he stuck like cactus to Angel. Their supplies and the picnic lunch were in a cooler that was attached to an extra tube which drifted along with them. Jack and Jonathan provided plenty of diversion to keep Dallas's efforts from being obvious. Of course, Adam was doing his part by being absolutely entranced with Honey Farrell. All in all, Dallas was well satisfied with the way things were turning out.

Angel was having the time of her life. She had never felt so carefree. She was draped across a huge black tractor tire tube, her fanny just dipping into the water. In fact, her feet, fanny, and fingertips were all that had gotten wet so far. The sun bathed her skin with warmth and she felt as lazy as a hound dog on a porch step. She laid her head back on the tube, eased her hands into the water, and let herself drift with the current.

Because of drought, the Frio River wasn't more

than knee-deep in most places. It was so crystal clear it was easy to see the bed of rocks and stones that formed the river bottom and explained the reason Dallas had told her to leave on her canvas tennis shoes during the float. Dallas complained that the low water level made the few rapids less fun. Angel thought they were plenty scary. At least with the lower water levels, the barbed wire that ranches had strung across the river to keep their stock confined was visible.

About an hour into the float Adam called, "Barbed wire ahead."

Angel stopped her tube and waited while Dallas held the barbed wire up so she could cross under it.

When she floated by him, he said, "Your legs are starting to get a little sunburned. We'd better stop and put some lotion on them."

Honey immediately stood up in the shallow water and stopped to wait for Dallas and Angel.

"You all go on ahead," Dallas said. "Angel and I will catch up."

"Are you sure?" Honey said. "We don't mind waiting."

Of course, that was a figurative *we.* The literal *we,* including Jack and Jonathan, were chomping at the bit and chafing at the delay.

"Go on ahead," Dallas urged. "We won't be long."

"If you're sure—"

Adam Philips cut Honey off when he took her tube out of her hand, set it back in the water, and said, "I'll hold this while you get settled."

Dallas was pleased with the flush that appeared at Honey's throat.

"Why, thank you, Adam," she said. "You're so kind."

Honey had a real Texas drawl, the slow, raspy kind that set a man's neck hairs to standing on end. Dallas could see it was working on Adam. Maybe he'd done his friend a good turn after all.

"You take the tube with the picnic supplies," Dallas said. "I've got the suntan lotion. We don't need anything else right now."

Dallas took his time dragging his and Angel's rubber tubes out of the water. When he finally joined her in the sun-sprinkled shade of the cypress trees that lined the bank, the other four tubes were out of sight around the bend.

"Shouldn't we hurry?" Angel asked.

"Naw," Dallas said. "We'll catch up." *By the end of the day.*

"If people nowadays wore more clothes, they wouldn't need suntan lotion," Angel pointed out.

"Yeah, but then we guys wouldn't have a

chance to do this to you gals.'' Dallas suited word to deed and began applying a handful of suntan lotion along Angel's smooth, bare leg.

Angel was mesmerized by the sight of Dallas touching her bare skin, by the pleasing roughness of his callused hand. Feelings went zooming in all directions. Up to her breasts, down to her belly and all points in between.

''Dallas,'' she said in a breathless voice.

''What, Angel?'' he murmured, completely absorbed by what he was doing.

''I think that's enough suntan lotion.''

''Yes, that leg's about done. I'll get the other one.''

Angel didn't think it was possible, but feelings started zooming all over again, as though her body hadn't just been through all this a minute ago. Angel's pulse was rocketing, her breath felt shortened as though she'd been running and her body felt discombobulated.

''Dallas, please stop.'' She reached down to grab his hand and was surprised when he twined his fingers with hers. She stared at their two hands, which he allowed to rest across her naked knees.

''Oh, my,'' Angel said.

''Yes. My thoughts exactly,'' Dallas said. He leaned forward and touched her lips with his. He had been waiting so long to kiss her again, it seemed like forever. Her mouth was unbearably sweet. And resilient. He felt his body tauten, his blood thrum. How could one simple kiss make him feel like this?

Angel moaned.

Dallas broke the kiss and leaned back far enough to see her eyes. She looked as stunned as he felt. Her cheeks were flushed, her eyes dilated and unfocused, her lips parted. He didn't intend to kiss her again, but he found the dewy wetness of her lips irresistible. He slowly closed the distance between them, waiting for some sign from her that she didn't want this.

It never came.

The sleek softness of her lips joined with his. Dallas deepened the kiss, all the time fighting to stay in control of it. The pleasure gathered in his loins, a slow, steady pulse of need. He took Angel's hand, the one entwined with his, and drew his across his chest and down across his belly. Her flesh felt exquisite against his!

Angel felt the crisp chest hair against the backs of her hands and the warmth of Dallas beneath her fingers. She rubbed her hand against his skin, wanting to touch him in ways she had only imagined in her dreams.

Dallas groaned, a guttural sound of need. His

other hand slid into Angel's hair and tightened, holding her captive for his kiss. His mouth ravaged, his tongue plundered. There was nothing controlled about the flash fire of need that tore through him, obliterating restraint. There was no chance now that she could escape his desire.

Not that Angel seemed in any hurry to get away.

When Dallas felt her tongue tentatively, delicately tracing his lips, he stilled his own tongue and opened his mouth to her. His heart was pounding. It was torture waiting for her, knowing she might change her mind and withdraw.

Angel felt as if she were on the edge of a precipice and that any second she would fall into space. She slid her tongue along Dallas's upper lip, as he had done to her, and slowly, cautiously, slipped it into his mouth. She touched his teeth and tongue, then retreated.

"Angel," Dallas murmured. "More, please."

He waited for her to come back with the same uncertainty he felt watching a butterfly that tempts and teases before finally lighting—or fluttering away.

His patience was rewarded.

When she broached his lips this time, his tongue greeted hers and withdrew, enticing her farther inside.

Angel's whole being was focused on the sensations created as she tasted Dallas and he returned the favor. She shuddered with pleasure and angled her mouth for better access.

When he first bit her lower lip, she was startled by the pain. The rush of pleasure that followed as he soothed it with his tongue was so intense she moaned deep in her throat. He taught her how to excite them both with love bites on her lips and throat and ears. His mouth was warm, his breath moist. She shivered. And shivered again.

Somehow her hands had flattened against his chest and she indulged the need to hold him, to touch him, to feel the textures of hair and skin. The first time her fingertips brushed across his nipple it was an accident. His response was immediate and telltale. The softness became a hard bud that was sensitive to her touch. She felt him tauten when she brushed against him the second time.

Entranced with his response, she played with him until, with a ragged voice he said, "Would you like me to do that to you?"

Angel froze. An arrow of pleasure shot from her breasts to her belly at the mere thought of his hands on her in so provocative a place. Before she could form words of consent or protest, Dallas's thumb had brushed lightly across the cotton T-shirt, creating a hard bud beneath it.

"Oh, my," Angel said.

"Yes. My thoughts exactly," Dallas rasped back.

Angel stiffened slightly and Dallas let his hand drop. She wasn't sure what to do. Her body was urging her to further exploration. Her mind was telling her she was an idiot to be playing with fire when she could get burned.

But Angel craved the warmth Dallas offered, and she had great confidence in her ability to take care of herself. She was in complete control of the situation. At least she was until Dallas reached up to cup both her breasts in his hands.

Angel gasped, and her eyes jerked up to meet his eyes, which glowed with arousal.

"You feel so good," he murmured, his thumbs lazily stroking her through the cotton T-shirt.

She grabbed his wrists, but not to push him away. She wanted his hands to stay right where they were.

"Dallas?" She didn't know what she was asking for. She was certain Dallas did.

Dallas knew, all right. He eased Angel back until she was lying beneath him. He mantled her body with his, easing himself between her thighs so she could feel the evidence of his desire. He nudged her once with his hips, and was satisfied with the responsive flare of excitement in her eyes.

He watched her as he caressed her body, saw her blue eyes darken and grow heavy-lidded with pleasure. He touched her shoulders and she lifted up to him. He caressed her ribs and felt her arch beneath his body. As he traced a hand across her belly, she sucked it in until her hipbones stabbed at him. Her arms circled round his neck, slipped up into his hair, and clutched him for dear life.

Dallas wanted to go slow, to savor everything with her, knowing it was the first time a man had touched her like this. But he was driven by a fever of need that made him demand what she had to give.

Angel wasn't able to think coherently. She was too busy feeling. Needing. Wanting. While Dallas trailed lavish kisses down her neck, her lips found the salty skin at his shoulder. She was entranced with the differences between them, his strength, his maleness, the hard, ropey muscles that bunched when she touched him. She wanted to feel bare skin against bare skin.

She had opened her mouth to speak when the raucous sounds of teenage voices reached them from the river.

"Way to go, man!"

"All *right!*" Followed by a shrill wolf whistle. "Yeah! Do it!"

Angel sat upright as though someone had pushed a button on a spring. When she would have jumped up and run, Dallas grabbed her and pulled her into his lap, her face against his chest, hiding her identity from the teenagers.

In moments the current had carried them away. Angel was still trembling with the realization of what might have happened if someone hadn't come along.

For his part Dallas could have cheerfully strangled the three teenage boys. He settled for a grin and a hearty wave as they disappeared around the bend.

When they were gone he said, "I'm sorry that happened." He paused and amended, "That came out wrong. What I meant is that I'm sorry you were embarrassed. It's so quiet here that I forgot about the rest of the world. I'm not at all sorry for anything else that happened."

Angel kept her face hidden against his chest as she admitted, "I'm not sorry, either."

Dallas found her chin and tipped it up so she was looking into his eyes. His voice was intense, urgent when he spoke. "I wish we were alone, Angel, with no one to interrupt us. I want to feel my hands on your skin, all over. I want to kiss you in places that will turn your face pink. I want to be inside you.''

Angel's lids lowered to hide what his words were doing to her. Could she really contemplate doing what he was asking? Without the benefit of marriage or any commitment from either of them? Without words of love?

''I...I want that, too,'' she said. ''But—''

Dallas put his fingertips on her lips to stop her. He didn't want to hear the words he knew were coming. She wanted to know whether he loved her. Whether the things they would do in bed together meant something more than the simple pleasures of the moment. She was right to ask. She was entitled to more than just a quick toss in the hay. But that was all he was prepared to offer her.

''We'd better get going,'' Dallas said. ''If we don't hurry there won't be much left of that picnic lunch.''

Angel felt bereft as Dallas pulled her to her feet and handed her one of the tractor tubes. He couldn't have made himself more clear if he'd shouted it from the rooftops. He didn't want complications in his life. And she was a complication.

The rest of the float might have been uncomfortable if Dallas hadn't thought up a game for them to play, a sort of ''most embarrassing moments'' kind of thing, where they were supposed to exchange lighthearted stories.

"You go first," Angel said.

"All right. Here goes. My most embarrassing moment occurred on my first date."

"How old were you?"

"Thirteen. I had a date with Jenny Haggerty, who I thought was the prettiest girl in junior high."

"Where did you take her?"

"To the movies. She lived on Main Street in Uvalde, so after my dad dropped me off at her house we walked downtown to the theater. We sat in the back row, so it would be really dark."

Angel chuckled. "Don't tell me you had evil designs on the poor child!"

"Devilish, sinful, lustful teenage boy-type designs," Dallas affirmed.

"And?"

"Our braces got locked together." Dallas waited for her laughter, and when it didn't come, looked at Angel. She had a quizzical expression on her face.

"Your suspenders got locked together? Why were you both wearing suspenders? I don't understand."

Dallas roared with laughter at the mistake she'd made. "They were dental braces," he said between guffaws. "Metal wires worn in our mouths for straightening our teeth."

Angel couldn't fathom such a thing. However, her smile grew as she realized how their braces must have gotten locked. "How did you finally get separated?" she asked.

"That's the really funny part," Dallas said, his eyes crinkling with merriment. "Doc Sheedy, the orthodontist, was seeing the same movie. He found us standing outside the theater after the show, terrified of what our fathers were going to say. He took pity on us, drove us to his office and untangled us without saying a word to our parents. I'll never forget the grin on his face when he warned me not to be kissing any more girls with braces until mine were off."

"How long before you were kissing girls again?" she asked.

"About a week," Dallas admitted with a grin. "But I was careful never to date another girl with braces."

She shook her head. "How different things are now. I never kissed a man until I was eighteen."

"Oh, and who was that?" Dallas was aware of a curious antagonism in his voice, but he couldn't do anything about it.

"James Peabody."

"With a name like that, I bet he was tall, gawky and had a big Adam's apple."

"He was short, stout and had a big Adam's apple," Angel admitted ruefully. "I met him on the docks in Galveston."

"What were you doing in a place like that?"

"Salvaging things."

Dallas cocked a brow.

"All right." She grinned. "Stealing. James Peabody was a night watchman. He caught me with a crate of chickens. I traded him a kiss for my freedom."

Dallas's eyes had gone hard and cold. "What else did he ask for?"

"It doesn't matter," Angel said. "The kiss was all he got. It wasn't much, as kisses go, just a peck on the lips. I broke away and ran before he could think to grab hold of me."

"It was a dangerous life you lived, Angel."

She laid her head back and stared at the clouds floating by. The sky was big and blue and looked the same as it had a century ago. "I wasn't unhappy, Dallas. I loved the challenge of living by my wits. I didn't have much to lose except my drawings. I bartered them occasionally for a sandwich and a piece of pie. A kiss was little enough to trade for my freedom."

"Didn't you ever want to settle down, marry a man and have some kids?"

"I thought about it," Angel said. "Sometimes, when I'd be alone in the middle of the prairie, with only a campfire to keep me company, I'd wish I could set down roots and start a family."

"Why didn't you?" Dallas asked.

"After Stephen was killed, I never met another man I cared about." *And now that I have, he isn't the marrying kind.* "How about you? Haven't you ever wanted to marry and have a family?"

"I told you what happened with my mother."

"So?"

"So I'm not about to repeat my father's mistake."

"Every woman isn't like your mother, Dallas. I'd think you would have realized that by now."

"Maybe they're not," he agreed. "But I wouldn't bet on it."

"How did you get so bitter and cynical?"

"Having one's mother walk out without a backward glance can do that to a person."

"It didn't affect me that way."

Dallas reached out and grabbed Angel's hand and pulled their tubes closer together. "I thought you told me you were orphaned. Are you saying your mother left you?"

"Actually she got caught stealing to feed us

and had to go to jail. Belinda and I ended up at the Orphans' Home in Galveston. She promised she'd come back for us when she got out of jail." Angel paused. "But she never did."

"Lord, I'm sorry, Angel."

"I never blamed her for leaving us there, Dallas. She did the best she could. I believe she loved us—me and Belinda. But she wasn't strong. Being in that orphanage made me strong, maybe stronger than I would have been if I'd stayed with my mother. I suppose I'll never know for sure. But I would never leave someone I loved. I couldn't do it. You can see that, can't you?"

He wanted to believe her. How simple things would be if he could believe her! But it wasn't easy to discard nearly two decades of distrust. "You think so now, Angel. What happens when things get tough?"

She smiled at him. "I've fought Comanches, buried my fiancé, and watched men shot to ribbons in the war. I've stolen to live, and I've run from the law. Does life in this world get any tougher than that?"

He smiled ruefully. "I see what you mean." Angel had given him a lot to think about. He used the rest of the float trip to consider what she had said. He had never thought he would be willing to risk trusting another woman. But somehow he no longer considered the risk of heartbreak greater than the possible joy of having Angel in his life. She filled a hole he hadn't realized was there until she had come into his life.

"Hey, there, slowpokes!" Adam called. "About time you showed up. We've already been upriver to retrieve your truck. There's some fried chicken left and a little watermelon, but that's about all."

Dallas took Angel's tube from her as she started up the bank to join Adam, Honey and the two boys.

"I didn't realize how hungry I was until you announced the food is nearly gone," Angel said with a grin. "Where's the chicken?"

While Honey helped Angel fill a plate with food, Adam helped Dallas put the last of the tubes into the pickup.

"Tell me," Adam asked, "did you have a nice trip?"

"Did you?" Dallas countered.

"Honey agreed to go to the opera in San Antonio with me next weekend."

Adam seemed to be seeking Dallas's approval. Dallas was more than willing to give it. "I think that's great. Honey loves all kinds of music."

Adam heaved a sigh of relief. "I thought…"

"I'm Honey's friend. I always will be. Nothing more."

"I'm still confused, though, about why you wanted me to ask Angel out on a date. Would you care to explain that to me?"

"I'd be glad to." *As soon as I understand it myself.* Suddenly Dallas decided just to tell Adam the truth—about everything. "Actually I have a confession to make."

"Oh?"

"You see, Angel isn't from around here."

"Whereabouts is she from?" Adam asked.

"She's from the past—1864 to be exact, and—"

Adam's laughter cut Dallas off. He clapped his friend on the back. "Angel's good for you," he said. "She's really improved your sense of humor."

"I'm telling you the truth," Dallas protested.

"Yeah, and I'm really a vampire," Adam said, pulling back his lips to expose nonexistent fangs.

"Why won't you believe me? I went into this cave on my property and when I came out on the other side of it there she was, surrounded by these six men and—"

"Lay off, Dallas. Just admit you love the woman. Now *that* I'd believe."

Dallas stared in bemusement as Adam walked

off chuckling. Adam's pronouncement was absurd. *Dallas Masterson in love?* Now *that* was farfetched!

11

—————

Dallas stared in awe at one of Angel's pen and ink drawings. It was a portrait of Belinda. He could easily see why Angel's gallery showing here in Houston was such a stupendous success. When she had told him—was it only four months ago?—that she did "a little drawing," he had never imagined this kind of talent. Each sketch he'd seen had possessed a poignancy, a sense of pathos, that moved him.

Angel's works depicting the past included: the portrait of Belinda standing outside the brothel where she worked; a very handsome young man—who had turned out to be Angel's fiancé—on the day he left for war, proudly outfitted in his Confederate uniform; and a dozen soldiers, with amputated arms and missing legs, slight wounds and terrible ones, waiting at a train station for the long ride home. Each sketch told a story. The joy and pain of a world long past were truthfully, sometimes brutally, reflected.

That same honesty was apparent in Angel's

sketches of modern subjects. She had done a portrait of Honey Farrell tubing down the Frio, her mouth curved in laughter, her eyes sad and wistful. There was a drawing of Dallas working with Jack and Jonathan at the corral. He and Jonathan were both wearing bandannas tied around their foreheads. Jack's bandanna was slipping out of his back pocket. Angel had faithfully recorded both Jack's animosity and Jonathan's adoration. Dallas's eyes, as he met Jonathan's gaze, were soft with a tenderness and concern he was embarrassed to have anyone see. How had she known so much about what each of them was feeling? More to the point, how had she captured those emotions so well on paper?

There was also a self-portrait. Angel was backed up against the cave entrance where Dallas had first seen her, peering into the darkness, of which she was so afraid. Meanwhile, six formless hulking shapes held her hostage. There was nothing timid or helpless about the woman she had drawn. Chin up, fists bunched, legs spread—it was a portrait of defiance, of determined independence. Nor was it fear he saw reflected on Angel's face as she contemplated the darkness within the cave. She had drawn the image of a man, half-formed, a point of light in the darkness. Angel's gaze was focused on the light, not the darkness surrounding it. Her eyes were filled with yearning and with hope.

"They're marvelous, aren't they?"

Dallas turned to find Ray Collinsworth at his shoulder. "Yes, they are."

"You must be very proud of Angel. Not only are her works a commercial success, but the critics love them. Her gift is extraordinary. She's going to be a very successful artist. And a very rich young lady."

"I want to thank you for helping Angel arrange all this." Dallas gestured to the pen and ink sketches mounted on the gallery walls. "And apologize for the way I behaved when—"

"It's not necessary. I'd have acted the same way if someone tried to move in on my woman. Angel's something pretty special. I envy you."

There was an awkward silence during which Dallas tried to decide whether to tell Ray Collinsworth that Angel wasn't "his" woman. Before he could say anything, Ray was called away by someone who wanted to rave over Angel's art.

Dallas searched the room, looking for Angel, and found her surrounded by a group of admirers. She was wearing a dress that Honey Farrell had helped her buy. It was sleeveless and strapless, and the bodice of the red satin fabric cupped Angel like a glove. But then, so did the rest of the dress. Her waist was tiny, her hips flared. He had spent a great deal of the evening imagining what it would be like to unzip the back of that dress and peel it off her.

She looked distant and elegant, not at all like the Angel he knew. He wanted to take her out of here, back to his ranch. And keep her there. But the woman of the past had made her way very well in the future. She didn't need him anymore.

It was a good thing he hadn't given his heart to her. She'd have broken it when she left him. As it was, he was going to miss her, but he wouldn't be devastated by the loss. At least, that's what he told himself.

Angel could feel Dallas staring at her. She wanted to go to him, to share her excitement and joy at the success of her drawings. She couldn't believe people would pay so much for pen and ink sketches. Ray Collinsworth had told her that the few pieces of art sold tonight had earned her thousands of dollars.

"The gallery wants as many drawings as you can produce," Ray had said.

Angel felt overwhelmed. "I can't believe this."

"Believe it," he said. "You're going to be financially independent, able to draw what you want, when you want."

Of course that was wonderful news, but her

feelings were mixed. The sale of her sketches and the request for more, meant that she had the means to support herself. If she wanted to, she could afford an apartment of her own, a car, a television, a microwave—in short, all the necessities of modern-day life. But Angel didn't want those things. Not if it meant leaving Dallas.

Her needs were simple: she wanted to settle down with Dallas and raise a family. She wanted to be his wife.

However, it was going to be an uphill battle convincing Dallas that she wasn't going to start looking for greener pastures the first chance she got. She had to convince him that so long as they were together, she would be happy.

She looked for Dallas and found him standing in front of her self-portrait. So far he hadn't said anything about whether he liked her sketches. She wanted him to like them. She worried that he wouldn't. But the bottom line was that she would still draw, whether he liked her work or not.

She made her way over to him, stopping to chat along the way. He looked so different in a tuxedo. His tanned complexion stood out against the stark white of the pleated shirt. He looked imposing and unapproachable. Not at all like the Texas Ranger who came home each day in a white yoked shirt, tan gabardine trousers, western belt and boots. He was still standing by the self-portrait when she reached him.

"Congratulations, Angel," he said. "Your exhibit is a big hit with everybody."

"Thank you."

"I'm really impressed. Your work is wonderful."

"You are? It is?" Angel couldn't help the smile that blossomed, lighting up her whole face.

"Did you think I wouldn't like it?" he asked.

"I hoped—I wasn't sure," she admitted. "I'm glad you do."

"When will you be leaving?" he asked.

"Leaving?" Angel felt stupid repeating the word, but she was shocked that he'd brought up the subject.

"Now that you have a career and can afford a place of your own, you'll be wanting to move on."

"I hadn't really thought about it," Angel said. She arched a brow. "Do you want me to move out?"

"I figured that's what you wanted."

"I have money for a place of my own, but I'm not sure where I want to go. Would you mind if I stay with you for a few more days until I make up my mind?"

Dallas shrugged. It was a stiff movement and

betrayed more than he wanted. "Sure. A few days is fine."

Angel didn't like the grim look on Dallas's face. Was it possible he didn't care? That she had only been a burden, and he was glad to be rid of her? She couldn't believe that. He cared. She knew he did. But she only had a few days to open his eyes to the fact that even though they had been born in different centuries, they had always belonged together.

She smiled up at him. "Thank you, Dallas. I appreciate your offer. When are we heading back to the ranch?"

"Early tomorrow, if that's all right with you. I've got reservations for us tonight—connecting rooms—at a hotel in town. Let me know when you're ready to go, and we can get out of here."

"I'm ready now," Angel said. The sooner she started her campaign, the better.

Their connecting rooms were on the sixteenth floor. The hotel lobby was an open space surrounded by rooms. The elevator was glass-enclosed and ran up an inside wall. Angel stared anxiously at it.

"Are you sure this won't fall?" she said as she stepped into it.

"I'm sure." Dallas smiled reassuringly and slipped her arm through his. In so many ways she was still an innocent. Who would be with her when she took her first airline flight? When she first laid eyes on the Grand Canyon? When she held her first child in her arms? He realized, with a start, that he wanted it to be him.

When they reached her room, he had trouble working the piece of plastic that the hotel had given him instead of a key to open the door.

"Here, let me," Angel said. She read the instructions, then calmly inserted the plastic card in the slot, waited for the light, removed the plastic, and opened the door.

She grinned at Dallas. "See? Easy as pie."

He stepped into the room with her. "Are you sure you know how to use everything?"

Angel surveyed the room. Telephone. Television. Refrigerator/Bar. Bathroom facilities. Bed. Chest. Lamps. Nothing strange. "I can manage," she said.

Dallas opened the connecting door between their rooms and crossed to his side. "If you need anything, just knock on the door. It won't be locked."

Angel felt her stomach clench as she walked over to close the door. Did she have the courage to cross over this threshold tonight? She had to find a way to let Dallas know she wanted him as more than a friend, that she wanted him as her husband. Would it help her cause, or hurt it, to approach him as a lover?

Dallas leaned over and kissed her softly on the mouth.

"Why did you do that?" she asked.

"Because you looked like you needed it."

"Dallas, I—"

"What, Angel?"

She wanted to ask him to make love to her. But the old moral values were hard to shed. "Thank you. I did need it. Good night." She closed the door behind him.

Dallas lay awake far into the night, aware of the light in Angel's room that kept away her dragons. She never had told him why she was afraid of the dark. Soon she would be leaving, and it would no longer be his problem. He should be glad to be done with the responsibility of her. He should be happy to be getting his privacy back.

Instead, Dallas felt a terrible sense of aloneness. Without the woman who had come to him from the past, his future seemed bleak and empty. He didn't have much time to convince her to stay. But he'd be damned if he let her stroll out of his life without lifting a hand to stop her!

Angel wasn't sure what woke her. She opened her eyes to total darkness. She reached for the lamp and turned the switch. Apparently the bulb had burned out. She told herself to stay calm. She would just get up and turn on the bathroom light. When she flipped the switch, nothing happened. The dark was frighteningly complete. Angel felt her way to the door that lead to the lobby and opened it, expecting to see light, but everything was black and silent.

"Don't get excited," she told herself. "Maybe they turn the electricity off in the middle of the night, maybe—" But she couldn't imagine such a thing.

It didn't take her long to find her way to the connecting door. The instant she opened it, she heard the covers rustle on the bed.

"Angel, is that you?"

"Yes. The lights won't turn on."

Dallas tried the lamp beside his bed, then got up and checked the bathroom light. "The electricity's out."

"How is that possible?"

"Brownout maybe. The main power source gets overloaded," he explained. "Everything cuts off."

"I…could I stay here with you until it comes back on?"

Dallas hesitated. He couldn't see Angel, but he knew what she'd packed to sleep in—one of those large, flimsy T-shirts he had bought the first week she'd come to stay with him. He was wearing only a pair of briefs. Before he could warn her that he wasn't dressed, she'd already found him in the dark and walked right into his arms.

Angel clung to Dallas as though he were a lifeline. She felt safe. "I'm so glad you're here," she murmured. "I don't fear the dark when I'm with you."

Dallas was doing everything in his power to control his raging hormones that had him as hard as a teenage kid in the back seat of a '57 Chevy. It wasn't working.

"Don't let go!" Angel said when he tried to release her. "Please. Just hold me."

Dallas pulled her back into the shelter of his arms and told his raging hormones to take a hike. But they weren't going anywhere without taking him along. Dallas felt Angel's breasts, soft against his chest, felt her fingers roam his back, smelled the fresh scent of herbal shampoo in her hair. Maybe if they got into bed she wouldn't have to hold on quite so tight.

"Let's go back to bed," he suggested.

"All right."

She walked beside him, aligning herself to his body, her head beneath his chin, her arm around his waist, her hip bumping against his.

A man could only take so much. He turned her in his arms and kissed her. Slow and deep. He felt banked coals burst into flame. His hands slid urgently down her back and curved around her buttocks, lifting her and pressing her hard against his arousal.

"Angel. I want you. I need you."

He never gave her a choice, just swept her into his arms and found his way to the bed. He laid her down and followed her with his body, fitting them together as he had longed to do. His mouth found hers in the dark, to still any protest. One of his hands caught both of hers above her head and held her captive, while the other hand shoved her flimsy T-shirt up and out of his way. He groaned when he realized she wasn't wearing anything—at all—under the shirt.

Then he was suckling her, teasing first one breast and then the other, until she was moaning and writhing under him. He kissed his way down her belly, to the portal below and kissed her there, too.

"Dallas, no. You can't—" She struggled against his hold.

"Don't be afraid," he murmured. "I only want to bring you pleasure. I won't hurt you. And I'll stop if you don't like it." He let her hands go and she grasped his hair.

Angel's whole body was tense, taut as a bowstring. He kissed her again, his tongue darting inward to the soft nether flesh, evoking feelings she had never expected, never even suspected she could feel.

"I want to feel everything, do everything with you, Dallas. I want—" Angel felt her body tauten as his kisses deepened, as he caressed her with teeth and tongue. The tension increased until she couldn't talk, couldn't breathe, couldn't *move*. A hoarse, animal sound forced its way out of her mouth. The pleasure was so intense it was almost painful. She writhed against his hold, fighting the sensations, fighting the loss of control.

"Don't fight it! Let it carry you away. *Feel* it!"

Angel clutched at Dallas as her body surged toward the ecstasy he had promised. She cried out as she felt herself pulled under, and succumbed wholly to the tremors that shook her.

She didn't know how long she lay quiescent, unaware of her surroundings. She became conscious gradually of Dallas's bristly cheek against her belly. Of his callused hand smoothing over her breast. Of her hands entwined in his hair, holding him close.

"I...I don't know what to say," she murmured.

He chuckled. "I think your body already said it for you."

"I...you didn't...we didn't..."

"The night isn't over yet." Dallas turned his face and kissed his way back up to her throat. He threaded his hands into her silky hair and held her still for his kiss.

She could taste herself faintly on his lips. Then their tongues mingled, and he began to mime the thrust of lovers joined. She pictured them together, their bodies linked, and her hips lifted to him. He cradled himself between her thighs, and she felt the hardness of him, rubbing against her, teasing the sensitive flesh he had so recently kissed.

"Dallas, please."

He didn't join their bodies right away. Instead, his hand slipped down between them, touching her intimately, his thumb stroking, his finger slipping inside her.

Angel should have felt embarrassed. She didn't. She wanted him to touch. Everywhere. Everything. She arched toward him, signaling her desire, and he put another finger inside her. Angel froze, aware of the feeling of fullness, of being stretched for the larger part of him that was yet to come.

She smoothed her hands through his hair, slid them down his back and felt the taut muscles in his buttocks. "Now," she urged. "Come into me now."

She lifted her hips, opening to him, but he didn't take her all at once. Instead, he merely put the soft tip of himself against her and teased his way slowly inside. She felt the barrier give way as she lost her innocence. At last Dallas thrust inside, filling her. She heard his groan of satisfaction and smiled.

Dallas's every thought was for Angel's pleasure. He couldn't help the fact that everything he did for her doubled his own enjoyment. Until finally, when he was seated deep within her, he knew it was too late to worry about losing his heart. It had long since been forfeited.

He loved her with his body and with his soul. He gave a part of himself he had never thought to share with any woman. And found himself enveloped in love.

Dallas shuddered as he climaxed, conscious of filling her with his seed, claiming her for all time, now and forever.

It was a long time before either of them had enough breath to speak, let alone strength to move. At last Dallas levered himself off Angel and pulled her into his arms. He laid a possessive hand across her breasts and dared her to deny him.

Angel had no intention of doing any such thing.

She inched herself back into the curve of Dallas's body and settled down for the night.

Neither of them had spoken a word of love. Neither of them had mentioned commitment. Yet both of them struggled mightily to figure out how it could be done.

"I think we should talk," Dallas said at last.

"All right. What do you want to talk about?"

Dallas opened his mouth to say *marriage* and couldn't get the word out. "Will you tell me why you're afraid of the dark?"

Angel grasped at the chance to avoid confronting the real issue between them. "The matron at the orphanage where I grew up left me in the root cellar as a punishment for stealing. The things I couldn't see turned into monsters in the dark. In the past anything I could see I could handle. What I couldn't see terrified me."

"That's how I've always felt about getting involved with a woman," Dallas murmured. "I could handle the physical relationship. What you see is what you get. But falling in love, giving my heart... It was too dangerous. How can you be sure that a woman loves you as much as you love her? How can you be sure you won't end up getting hurt?"

"I don't know," Angel admitted reluctantly. "I still haven't gotten over my fear of the dark. But

I haven't let it stop me from living a full life. I simply light a candle and make a safe place for myself in the darkness."

Dallas smiled against the back of her neck. "Will you be my candle in the darkness, Angel?"

"Is that a proposal?"

He felt his throat thicken and swallowed painfully. "I love you, Angel. Will you marry me and live with me and bear my children?"

She answered him with a kiss, a timeless sort of thing. It didn't feel like the past or the present or even the future. It felt like endless love.

She leaned over to kiss Dallas full on the mouth. It was an even sweeter thing to love him now, knowing that they were committed to each other. She let her hands roam down his chest to his belly and beyond.

Dallas groaned. "Angel..."

"What?"

"You're killing me."

"You don't like it?"

"I love it."

"Then shut up and enjoy it." She trailed her fingers along his thigh and belly.

He groaned again.

"So that feels good?"

He slid his own hand into the same spot on her body.

Angel gasped. "Oh, my."

"My thoughts exactly," he grated. His callused hands were rough against her skin, tantalizing, teasing. His mouth found hers and he mimed with his tongue the ageless act of love.

Angel gasped for air when his mouth slid to her ear and he teased it with his tongue. Her hands grasped for flesh and locked on his shoulders. Crescents appeared in the golden flesh as she moaned her delight.

"Dallas," she said breathlessly. "I love you."

Angel waited for him to say the words in return. When they didn't come right away, she stiffened, afraid he couldn't say them because he didn't feel the same way about her as she did about him.

Dallas sensed Angel's withdrawal and lifted his head to meet her eyes. He felt a lump in his throat that made it hard to speak. But speak he must.

"I love you, Angel. I think I have for a long time." He kissed her eyes and said, "I love you." Then he mouthed the words against her lips. "I love you."

The more he said it, the easier it was to say it. The lump eased as he saw the blazing smile on her face, the happiness in her slumberous blue eyes.

"Love me, Angel."

"You don't have to ask," she whispered.

It took a matter of moments to join them, one with the other. How good it felt to be together this way. As though they always had been, as though they always would be.

Dallas moved slowly at first, making sure he wasn't hurting Angel and that she was keeping up with him. He didn't want to leave her behind. But he needn't have worried. For soon, Angel's urgency forced him to greater heights of pleasure, until he couldn't wait any longer.

"Angel, I can't—"

"Dallas, I—"

They reached together for the pinnacle of pleasure and found it. The woman from the past. The man of the future. Making together a child of the present.

"Don't move," Angel said after he had spilled his seed within her. "I don't want it to end."

"I'm too heavy."

"It feels good. Please."

He stayed as he was, his head relaxed on her breast, their bodies still joined. As their skin cooled, he levered himself off her and pulled the covers up over them. He drew her into his embrace, thanking whatever gods of fortune had taken him into the cave and brought her into his life from another time.

"I love you," Angel murmured.

"Go to sleep, wife," he said.

It sounded good. It sounded fine. It sounded like forever.